KU-348-371

FOR MY MOTHER.

WHAT AN ADVENTURE IT HAS BEEN.

&

FOR TRANS, NONBINARY, GENDER-CREATIVE,

AND GENDER-FIERCE YOUTH.

YOU ARE SEEN. YOU ARE PRECIOUS.

AND YOU ARE SO, SO LOVED.

One

Spencer's morning went to hell when some asshole on a dirt bike swerved in front of Mom's Subaru.

Mom slammed on the brakes and flung her arm across Spencer's chest, despite the fact that he was wearing a seat belt, and even if he weren't, it's not like her arm would keep him from hurtling through the windshield and becoming sausage meat.

At least she'd already finished her coffee. The last thing he needed was to spend all day smelling like the inside of a Starbucks.

"Is everyone okay?" Mom twisted around to check on Theo in the back seat, but his eyes remained glued to the nature show playing on his tablet. Spencer was impressed by how nothing seemed to faze his little brother.

"Maybe we save the vehicular manslaughter for tomorrow," said Spencer. He didn't want to be known as the kid whose mom ran over someone at drop-off. He wasn't sure he wanted to be known as *anything*. As far as he was concerned, the less he stood out, the better.

Mom ignored him as she steered the car more carefully up the tree-lined drive and parked at the curb. "Promise me you'll make an effort today. Talk to people. Smile sometimes." She tugged on one of his earbuds, pulling it out of his ear. A muffled *da-da-da-dun-da-da-da-dun* from the song he was listening to trickled out into the car. "It wouldn't kill you to be more social."

"It might."

Mom's jaw clenched. "That's not funny, Spencer. Not after last year."

"Too soon?" said Spencer. If he turned it into a joke he could pretend that he didn't still wake up in the middle of the night, heart racing, drenched in sweat thinking about The Incident. He called it "The Incident" so he wouldn't have to remember it all in excruciating detail: the threatening email, the picture of his face in crosshairs stuffed in his locker, the call to the school that prompted a lockdown, huddling in the corner of a dark classroom, the cold tile leeching heat from his body, and knowing that if someone got hurt, it would be all his fault.

"I'm serious, Spence. We don't have other options if this doesn't work."

"I know. I'm sorry." The back of his neck grew hot and prickly like it had whenever he was awakened in the small hours of the day by the creak of the staircase as Dad crept up to bed after spending all night preparing for the extra college courses he was teaching that summer to pay for Spencer's tuition.

Even with the extra work, it didn't take a math genius to figure out that Dad's paycheck was barely enough to send one kid to private school, let alone two. So after two years in a Montessori program his little brother, Theo, who was autistic, had to go to public school for the first time.

Theo had spent his summer stretched out on the living room carpet in front of the TV watching anything and everything with the word *planet* in the title. Spencer wasn't sure how well an encyclopedic knowledge of the mating behavior of amphibians (called *amplexus,* according to Theo) would go over with other eight-year-olds.

"Hey, what's with the face?" asked Mom. "This is going to be a great year. For both of you," she added, reaching around to pat Theo on the knee.

Spencer picked his backpack up off the floor and squeezed it to his chest. He reached out to open the door when Mom said, "Are you sure you want to keep that there?" She pointed at the *I'm here, I'm queer, get over it* pin on the front pocket.

Spencer's fingers brushed over the pin. He'd had the same conversation with Aiden over the phone last night.

"Think of it as a test," Aiden had said. "If someone makes a big deal out of it, you'll know to steer clear. Besides, how else will you find the other queers?"

"I'm just saying," continued Mom, "it's a bit . . . provocative for your day one. Why don't you wait and see how the QSA meeting goes first? That's today, right?"

Spencer nibbled his bottom lip. Last night he had agreed

with Aiden, but now, seeing the glittery, rainbow letters sparkling in broad daylight, the idea of walking into the building with it on felt like sticking a target on his back. Sure, Oakley might brag about being the most liberal school in the county—after all, that's why they'd chosen it—but it was still in rural Ohio, where just that morning they'd passed by half a dozen churches, one of which had a sign that said: *Don't be so open-minded your brains fall out.*

He undid the clasp and tucked the pin in his backpack, hoping Aiden didn't ask him about it when they debriefed after school.

"All right, do you know where you're going?" asked Mom.

"I think so," he mumbled.

"If you're not sure, you need to ask for directions."

"I know." He tried to keep the tinge of annoyance out of his voice. When Mom got anxious, she tended to treat him like a baby. But this was a big day for all of them.

"Here," said Mom. She rolled down Spencer's window, and leaned over him, calling, "Hey, you with the bike!"

Spencer slouched lower in his seat as several kids, including the boy on the dirt bike, turned to stare at them.

"Mom, what are you doing?"

The boy on the bike reversed, rolling backward to the car and stopping outside Spencer's window.

"I'm sorry about cutting you off earlier, ma'am. I didn't want to be late." His voice was low and gravelly and muffled inside his retro motocross helmet.

"That's quite all right," said Mom, clearly charmed by his slight Appalachian twang. Her own accent, courtesy of a childhood in West Virginia, came out stronger. "This is my son Spencer. He's new this year."

"Nice to meet you." The boy stuck a gloved hand through the window. The worn leather was as soft as a lamb's ear against Spencer's palm.

"Do you think you could show him to his first class?" asked Mom.

The helmet visor hid the boy's expression, but Spencer imagined the amusement in his face at being asked to play babysitter. "It's okay—" he began, longing to turn around, go home, and try again tomorrow, but then the boy lifted off his helmet and Spencer's words died in his throat.

He was cute—all farm boy tan in a navy polo and Wrangler's. But what really made Spencer's insides feel like he'd just been dematerialized and rematerialized in a transporter was that this kid, with his brown eyes and megawatt smile currently aimed right at Spencer, was a dead ringer for Wesley Crusher from *Star Trek: The Next Generation*.

Spencer's nightly ritual was watching *Star Trek* with his dad, who would disown him, not as a son but as a fellow Trekkie, if he knew that the only reason he put up with the cheesy special effects was because of his teeny-tiny crush on acting ensign, wunderkind, Wesley Crusher.

Mom gave him a little nudge. "I have to go put Theo on the bus. Have a good day, sweetie."

Spencer climbed out of the car, careful not to trip over himself, and slammed the door behind him. Did she have to call him sweetie? In front of *him*? What was wrong with bud? Or sport? Bike Boy's parents probably didn't call *him* sweetie, especially not at school.

He waved them off, watching the Subaru disappear around the corner, and trying to ignore the hollow feeling in his chest.

"So, what grade are you in?" asked the boy, parking his bike and waiting for Spencer on the sidewalk.

Spencer's thoughts became all tangled up in his head as he tried to shape them into words.

"Are you a first year?" Bike Boy prompted.

"No," said Spencer, a little too forcefully. He pulled himself up to his not very tall height of five feet. He wasn't insecure about it, not really, but it would be a long year if everyone, *especially* cute boys, thought he was a middle schooler who got lost on his way to class. "I'm a sophomore."

"Cool, me too."

He followed Bike Boy up the path to the gated entrance. On the way the boy waved to a couple kids and high-fived another, but he didn't introduce Spencer. Then again, what would he say? *This is the kid whose mom almost ran me over and then made me walk him to class*? Not exactly the first impression Spencer wanted.

"Let me guess, you were kicked out of your old school for

talking too much." Bike Boy shot Spencer a wide grin. His two front teeth overlapped slightly, which Spencer found oddly endearing considering that most of his friends had been put in braces as soon as they hit double digits.

Spencer searched for something witty to say back. Something to show Bike Boy that he wasn't a complete weirdo, but his words got lost again.

The smile on Bike Boy's face slipped off. "Wait, were you actually kicked out? I'm sorry, I—"

"I wasn't kicked out."

"It was just a joke."

"I know," said Spencer, growing frustrated that even the most basic of conversations left him flustered.

Not wanting to prolong the agony, he made a decision when they reached the entrance. He knew where he was going. Sort of. He had taken a tour earlier that summer when signing up for classes.

"So what's your first class?" asked Bike Boy.

He opened his mouth to respond when someone going past pushed him from behind, and he fell into Bike Boy, who reached out a hand to steady him.

Spencer pulled back his arm like he'd been burned. "It's okay. I know where I'm going. But thanks for your help."

Bike Boy searched his face as if trying to see if he was telling the truth. "Are you sure?"

Spencer nodded, scuffing his foot against the floor.

"All right, then. I'll see you around, I guess," said Bike

Boy, his voice lilting slightly like he was asking a question. He hitched his backpack higher and turned to join the swarm of students on their way to class.

Spencer watched him leave, not with relief, but with something that felt a little like guilt. Maybe he should be a touch nicer to the guy who had offered to help him, despite narrowly escaping death at the wheels of his mother's Subaru. Hell, Spencer didn't even know who he was.

Before he could stop himself, he called out, "Wait, what's your name?"

Bike Boy turned and flashed Spencer a smile. "Justice. Justice Cortes."

Justice Cortes. Spencer silently mouthed the name before another wave of students knocked into him. He shook his head. The last thing he needed was to think about Justice Cortes, or any boy, really.

What he needed was to keep his distance. If he didn't get too close to people, they wouldn't find out his secret. If they didn't find out, they couldn't use it against him. Nobody at Oakley knew he was transgender.

Spencer needed to keep his head down, study hard, and escape Apple Creek, population 1,172, where the only traffic jams were caused by tractors and Amish buggies.

But first he'd have to survive PE.

. . .

After a few wrong turns, he finally found the locker rooms just as the warning bell rang.

When he opened the door the nauseating stench of body spray mixed with floral air freshener blasted him in the face, invading his nostrils and making him light-headed.

Spencer hovered awkwardly at the door as a few stragglers in various stages of undress glanced up at him from the wooden benches lining the room. Maybe he should change in the nurse's bathroom like Ms. Greene, his guidance counselor, had suggested. Private stall, a door that locked, and nobody who'd snap him in half like a twig if given the chance. But then someone might wonder why he didn't change with the rest of them. First rule of passing: Don't be different.

He found an empty corner and untied his shoes, avoiding eye contact. He wiggled his toes as a chill from the concrete floor seeped through his socks. After a minute the only sounds in the locker room were the thumping of his heartbeat and the dripping of a leaky faucet.

Alone at last, he jumped into action, wriggling out of his jeans and pulling on shorts from his backpack. He tugged on his T-shirt, grateful, not for the first time, that he hadn't needed top surgery or to suffer through wearing a binder. Starting hormone blockers at thirteen prevented too much growth and almost one year on testosterone replaced whatever fat there was with smooth muscle.

The late bell rang and he slipped into sneakers, shoved his clothes and backpack into a locker, and hurried out the door.

With its towering oak trees and ivy-covered walls, the Oakley School looked impressive on the outside. But inside, the lemony scent of disinfectant and the squeak of his shoes against the linoleum as he jogged down the hallway connecting the locker room to the gym told Spencer that this was more like the charter school Miles Morales attended than the Xavier Institute. The hallway, which had teemed with the hustle and bustle of chattering students five minutes ago, was empty. He snuck into the gym, where a dozen or so boys were flinging foam balls at each other. One sped toward his face, forcing him to duck. Where was the teacher?

"You're late."

Spencer jumped and twisted around to see a man in a baseball cap standing beside him. The man wore saggy sweatpants and a ridiculous-looking cardigan with a hood—a hoodigan?—and had a toothpick dangling from his mouth.

"Are you Coach Schilling?" he asked, slightly out of breath. "Sorry, I—"

"Name?" Coach Schilling cut him off.

"Spencer Harris."

"Harris, eh?" He surveyed his clipboard, rolling the toothpick from one side of his mouth to the other.

Sweat pooled clammy and moist under Spencer's armpits.

The principal, Mrs. Dumas, had assured him that his school records would have the correct name and gender, but that didn't stop the panic rising in his chest. If someone had made a mistake, he'd be outed in his very first class, and all of it—his dad working overtime, Theo switching schools—would be for nothing.

"You're new," said Coach Schilling. It wasn't a question. With a school this small, new students must be easy to spot. "Make sure you're on time tomorrow." He pulled a magazine from the back of his sweatpants and began thumbing through it.

"Could you tell me what's going on?" Spencer sidestepped as another ball hurtled toward him.

Coach Schilling, preoccupied with uncovering the secret to getting rock-hard abs in thirty days, barely glanced up from his magazine and said, "Dodgeball."

"Right," said Spencer. "But what should I actually be doing?"

Coach Schilling raised a bushy eyebrow and gave three sharp bursts of his whistle. A hush fell across the gym. Spencer's face burned as all eyes turned on him. Coach Schilling picked up a loose ball and shoved it in Spencer's hands. "Take this and throw it over there." He pointed across the painted line in the center of the gym. "No head shots, no crotch shots. Got it?"

Spencer nodded.

"Good. Have fun." Coach Schilling blew his whistle to start the game then went to sit on the bleachers with his magazine.

Spencer's knees knocked together as he joined his teammates. At least if it was a total disaster he could probably duck out after attendance tomorrow and Coach Schilling wouldn't even notice.

After a few minutes of playing, Spencer's pent-up anxiety about the first day of school dripped away with the sweat. He might be small, but he was nimble on his feet. He ducked, dived, and even got in a few hits himself, until he was the last man standing on his team and found himself outnumbered, two to one.

His first opponent, a tall boy with shaggy brown hair, chucked a ball at him. Spencer did a clumsy pirouette and it whipped past. He grinned as his teammates called out encouragement from the sidelines.

His second opponent threw a ball, which Spencer caught. His team erupted into cheers as the player moved to the sidelines, out of the game. Now it was Spencer and the shaggy-haired kid.

The boy launched the ball into the air. Spencer used the ball in his hands to deflect it back, then threw his second ball, forcing the kid to defend both shots simultaneously.

To Spencer's shock, his opponent reached out with hands the size of Spencer's face and caught both balls. Spencer was out.

Coach Schilling blew his whistle. "All right, game over."

Spencer threw his head back. He didn't consider himself a sore loser, but he disliked losing enough to make sure it didn't happen very often. When it did, it was like a kick to the shins: incredibly painful, but unlikely to cause any real damage.

He forced his grimace into a smile as his opponent approached him, hand outstretched. "Nice moves out there, Twinkle Toes." He winked at Spencer.

Spencer's cheeks ached with the effort of keeping his smile from falling. He took the kid's hand, squeezing it limply. He couldn't tell if he was making fun of him or not.

As the kid turned around and started walking back to his buddies, Spencer's pulse raced. He imagined him telling them what he'd just called Spencer and the nickname spreading around the school. His eyes fell on a ball in front of him, and before his brain caught up with his body, Spencer pulled his leg back and let loose. The ball made a perfect arc in the air before smacking the kid in the back of his head.

The kid whirled around, his cheeks flushed and eyes flashing. Spencer's brain finally caught up. *Oh, shit.*

"Who did that?" shouted the kid.

All eyes turned to Spencer. Even the girls playing

badminton over on the other side of the gym with their own teacher stopped their game.

The kid rounded on Spencer.

Spencer flinched.

"Did you throw that at me?"

Spencer couldn't exactly lie, not with a room of witnesses. "No, I kicked it."

"With your right foot or your left foot?" asked the kid.

"I— What?" asked Spencer, wondering what the hell that had to do with anything.

The kid took another step toward Spencer, who found himself backed up against the wall. "That shot. Did you make it with your right foot or your left?"

"Left. My left."

To Spencer's surprise, the boy smiled and turned to Coach Schilling. "Did you see that, Coach?"

Coach Schilling was also staring at Spencer with a curious look on his face. "That I did, son, that I did." He paused, looking thoughtful. "Macintosh, why don't you head to the nurse and get an ice pack. You." He pointed his whistle at Spencer. "Harris, right?"

"Yes, sir," said Spencer.

"You're coming with me."

Two

If there were a record for fastest expulsion, Spencer had crushed it. Maybe he could do online classes or Mom could homeschool him again. That is, if she didn't kill him when she found out what he'd done.

He followed Coach Schilling into a dingy room the size of a broom closet. A whiteboard with scribbled, half-erased plays was stuffed in the corner.

Coach Schilling squeezed himself behind a tiny desk and indicated for Spencer to sit on a metal folding chair. Spencer was so cramped that his knees collided against the front of the desk, which was bare except for a framed photograph of a boy with a toothy grin holding a baseball bat, and a placard that said *Luck is for the Unprepared*, which wasn't helpful, as Spencer wasn't feeling lucky, nor prepared.

Coach Schilling steepled his fingers together and eyed Spencer. "I've got one question for you," he began, a huge grin spreading across his face. "Where the heck have you been all my life?"

"I—uh—what?" Maybe private school handled discipline differently.

"I'll give it to you straight: I need a player like you on my team."

"Your team?" He'd figured "Coach" was some sort of honorary title bestowed upon PE teachers after a certain number of years forcing kids to climb ropes and run a timed mile.

"Soccer, football, the beautiful game. Whatever you want to call it. Surely you've played before. I was watching you in dodgeball. You're agile and have an innate intelligence for finding space. And the way the ball collided with Macintosh's head tells me your shot has accuracy and power."

"Yeah, I used to play midfield." Thinking of his old team brought back warm memories of playing cards during long bus rides to games, and monthly chili dinners at his coach's house.

"We're neck deep in football country, which means I don't even have enough players for a separate JV team because they'd all rather get concussions fighting for a pigskin. I need someone like you if we have any chance at winning the League Cup this year."

Framed team photos lined the wall behind Coach Schilling. Row upon row of boys stared back at Spencer, the passage of time measured by their hair getting shorter and their shorts getting longer. He recognized his opponent from PE wearing the goalie kit in the most recent photo, which explained how he had blocked Spencer's shots. Then he found another familiar face in the lineup.

"That boy, there. He's still on the team?" he asked, doing his best to sound casual.

Coach Schilling followed to where he was pointing. "Ah, that's Justice Cortes. Sophomore. Scouted him myself. He also plays midfield."

Well, shit, that was just what Spencer didn't need. He'd barely been able to string two sentences together when he spoke with Justice earlier that morning, and that was when they were both fully clothed. He'd probably become completely comatose if he had to change in front of him.

Coach Schilling watched him expectantly. The thing was, he knew he was a boy, but he didn't know if he belonged on that wall of players with their broad shoulders and narrow hips. None of them had to worry about getting changed in the locker room or where to hide their tampons in case they started their period.

Besides, being on a team again and getting that close to people had risks. Worst of all, if everything went haywire, it wouldn't just be him who'd be affected. There was Mom, Dad, and Theo to think about.

On the other hand, that twenty minutes playing dodgeball was the first time in a long time that he felt like he belonged to something bigger than himself, like other people had his back. It was a nice feeling.

"I don't know," said Spencer.

Coach Schilling scratched his days-old stubble. "Well, you signed the handbook, so I assume you're familiar with our zero-tolerance policy for violence. Maybe Principal Dumas will be lenient on you since you're new, but zero tolerance generally means, well, zero tolerance."

Okay, that changed things. "And if I join?"

"When I fill out the incident report, I'll call it an accident."

Getting blackmailed by his PE teacher hadn't been part of his plans, but Coach Schilling's offer had to be better than whatever his parents would do to him.

"Can I think about it?"

Coach Schilling handed him a piece of paper. "Have your parents sign this. Tryouts are tomorrow after school."

By lunchtime, Spencer's brain was fit to bursting with all the information he had to remember from his morning classes: how to get to them, the names of his teachers, the page numbers for the homework he'd been assigned, even though it was only day one.

He slipped past the cafeteria, which sounded like it had been taken over by wild animals, and instead made his way to the classroom where the Queer Straight Alliance was meeting. He double-checked the number by the door, making sure it matched the one that Ms. Greene had sent in an email a few days ago. If he couldn't wear his pin, Spencer figured this was the next best method of meeting other queer students.

He steeled himself, then opened the door.

Inside, the desks had been arranged in a semicircle. Spencer counted six other students. It looked like he was the last to arrive.

A boy in a deep V-neck shirt and a pair of skinny jeans so tight they could have been painted on looked up at the sound of the door opening. "Here for the QSA? Come on in. we're about to do names and pronouns."

Spencer took a seat at the desk nearest to the door.

"I'll start," continued the boy. "My name is Grayson Condon and I use *he* and *him*. This is my third year at Oakley and my second year as president of the QSA." He turned to the kid slouched in a chair to his left.

"I'm Riley." Chin-length blond hair with purple streaks peeked out from under the kid's hoodie.

"And your pronouns?" asked Grayson.

Riley stared at the floor. "I . . . I don't know. I'm still figuring everything out."

Grayson leaned forward. "Hey, this is a safe space. You can use whatever pronouns you want here." He gave the kid a reassuring smile.

"*They,* I guess." Riley uncrossed their arms and sat up straighter.

"Okay, then, *they* it is. Let us know if anything changes."

Spencer nodded at Riley encouragingly. Coming out was never easy, even when it went well.

The first time he came out was in a Kroger parking lot when he was thirteen.

He had endured awkward puberty talks from his parents and his health teacher, and intellectually he knew that one day he'd grow boobs, and hips, and look like the women he saw on TV. But there was part of him that thought, *What if I didn't*.

Before he went to bed each night, Spencer would pray that he would wake up as a boy.

It never worked.

Then, one day when he was in eighth grade, one of his teammates came up to him after soccer practice. Even with a strand of hair stuck to her glossy lips, she carried herself with a sort of unself-consciousness that Spencer had never felt before. She was like everything a girl should be, and everything that Spencer wasn't.

"Look," she said, "this is awkward, but maybe you should think about wearing a sports bra. You can borrow one of mine if you want," she added, trying to be helpful. "I think it will really improve your game."

A red, hot tingle started to prickle Spencer's scalp and crawled down his back. There was no meanness in her comment, but the idea that someone had been inspecting his body, especially *that* part, made him feel sick. If she had noticed he needed a bra, then other people did too.

So, Spencer didn't show up for the next game. Then he skipped a few practices and stopped going to team sleepovers. He stopped doing much of anything.

One day Mom dragged him out of the house to the grocery store. As they were leaving, her phone rang. She pulled back into their parking spot to check the caller ID.

"Mom, can we go home? The ice cream is going to melt." He didn't really care about the ice cream, but he wanted to be back in his bedroom, the only place where he could truly be himself.

"You know I don't like talking and driving. It's your coach. This will only take a minute." She answered the phone.

Spencer took out his own phone to lose himself in an endless scroll through social media but was brought back when Mom's voice rose.

"Excuse me, what?" Mom swiveled in her seat to look at him. "I'm going to have to call you back." She hung up and frowned at Spencer. "Coach Ireland says you haven't been going to practice."

Spencer avoided her eyes. "Can we talk about this later?"

"No, we're talking about it now. Do you know how much money we spend for you to be on that team? I'm talking about your kit, gas to drive you to games and tournaments, that summer camp you went to. And you can't even be bothered to show up for practice? What's going on with you?"

Silence filled the car.

Mom spoke again. "Do you not want to play anymore?"

It was as if an ice cube were stuck in his throat. He shook his head.

"Then why didn't you tell me you wanted to quit soccer?"

"I don't want to quit soccer." Spencer's voice came out raspy. "I just don't want to play on that team. I want to play on a boys' team."

Mom drew in a breath. "I have to say, I'm disappointed. You know that girls play just as hard as boys." Leave it to Mom to turn his coming out into a speech about feminism.

"No, it's not that. It's just, I just—" He paused, unable to continue. "I don't think I'm supposed to be a girl." He stuffed his hands under his legs to stop them from shaking.

Mom stared straight ahead. "I don't understand."

He took a deep breath. "I don't want boobs."

"Sweetie, lots of girls feel that way. It's natural to be uncomfortable about your changing body."

"It's not just boobs. It feels wrong when I get my period."

"You got your period, when?"

"A couple months ago." He'd stuffed his underwear with a hand towel and thought that if he ignored it, it would go away.

She didn't say anything for a long while. Spencer's chest felt tight, like a cord had been wrapped around it. Then she said, "Thank you for telling me. I want you to know that I'll always love you, whether you feel like you're a girl or a boy or whatever." And the cord around his chest loosened.

A week later, they went to Supercuts for his first short haircut. Examining his fresh fade in the mirror afterward, he finally looked more on the outside how he felt on the inside.

One evening, not long after, Mom went out and Dad said she was meeting a friend. She came home late and knocked on Spencer's door. He was on his bed, his laptop on his thighs. She entered the room.

"Can I sit?"

Spencer moved his laptop, which had gotten too hot for his legs, and pulled his knees up to his chest.

"I went to a support group for parents of transgender and gender non-conforming kids. That's what you are, right?"

"I guess."

"There were a lot of nice people there who gave me some great advice. This is all new to me, so tomorrow I'm going to make an appointment for you to see a therapist who specializes in these types of issues and get you the support you need."

"Really?"

She put a hand on his knee. "I'm not going to make you grow up into someone you're not meant to be."

"Name and pronouns?" asked Grayson.

Spencer realized that the room had grown quiet and looked up to see everyone staring at him.

He swallowed; his throat felt like sandpaper. "I'm Spencer—"

"Can you speak up?" interrupted Grayson.

"Sorry," he said, louder. "My name's Spencer, I use *he, him, his*."

"Awesome, thanks Spencer," said Grayson.

When everyone had introduced themselves, Grayson took the floor again, sharing a bit more about the QSA and the different programs they did each year.

"We have to do something for National Coming Out Day in October. Then in November there's Transgender Day of Remembrance. And we always do something big for Pride before school ends in June. If you want to take the lead on planning anything, let me know."

The rest of the meeting passed smoothly, a welcome oasis from all the chaos that morning, and Spencer grew hopeful that maybe he'd found a place at Oakley where he could belong.

Still, Spencer was glad when the meeting ended early since it gave him the chance to use the bathroom before everyone else exited the cafeteria en masse. He even managed to find a stall where the toilet wasn't completely covered with pee. He quickly took care of business, then left, almost bumping into Riley outside the door.

"Sorry," he said, holding the door open for Riley.

Riley hesitated. Spencer read the anxiety in their face.

"There's nobody in there, if you want to go in now," he said.

Riley still looked unsure.

"I can wait outside and tell anyone who tries to go in that there's a leak or something."

Riley cracked a smile. "You'd do that?"

Spencer shrugged. "Of course." He leaned against the wall and waited, nodding awkwardly at people as they passed by. His anxiety spiked each time it was a guy. Still, it felt good to use his passing privilege to help Riley.

To Spencer's immense relief, no one tried to use the bathroom, and after a couple minutes Riley came back out.

"Thanks," they said, hanging their messenger bag across their shoulder. As Riley started down the hall, Spencer noticed a patch with Aiden's band name sewed to their bag. "Wait, you know The Testostertones?" he called out.

Riley turned back. "They're like my favorite band."

"No way. Aiden Nesbitt is one of my best friends," said Spencer excitedly.

"Seriously?"

"Yeah, I met him . . ." Spencer trailed off. He'd met Aiden at a two-week sleepaway camp for trans kids. But he wasn't ready to come out, not yet, even to Riley. "I met him this summer."

"Is he as awesome as he seems online?"

"Better." To be honest, Spencer often suspected that lots

of people considered Aiden to be their best friend. That's just who he was. It helped that he was the drummer in a punk rock band, ran an active YouTube channel documenting his transition, and had an internship at a popular online queer zine.

"If you want, I could introduce you sometime," said Spencer. "His band has a few gigs coming up. I could see if he can get us tickets; we could all hang out."

"That would be amazing," said Riley.

"Cool. Give me your number and I'll let you know." Spencer couldn't stop the smile spreading across his face as Riley punched their number into his phone. Maybe this whole making friends thing wouldn't be so hard after all.

Three

Music Appreciation was Spencer's last class, and the one he'd been looking most forward to. For the first time all day, he made it to class early. The classroom was deep in the school's basement. Guitars with chipped necks lined the wall and mismatched chairs were arranged in a semicircle.

The stained, mustard-yellow carpet and lack of natural lighting suggested to Spencer that his tuition money wasn't going toward funding the arts at Oakley. Especially when he compared this room to the state-of-the-arts science lab he'd seen during his tour of the school.

Mom had clutched his arm excitedly at the sight of it, her nails leaving half-moon–shaped indents in his skin. Spencer liked science. He was good at it, great even. The science fair medals pinned to the corkboard in his bedroom proved that. At his old school, he'd been allowed to take chemistry a year early.

But when he'd told her that he wanted to take Music Appreciation instead of physics, she acted like he'd said that he wanted to enroll in a Klingon language course instead of English.

"Do you really want to choose a music elective over science? That's not like you, Spence."

The thing about moms is that they think they understand you better than you do yourself, just because they changed your diaper for a couple years.

Along with an affinity for science, Spencer also inherited his mom's complete lack of musical talent. Dad, on the other hand, still slept in the T-shirt from his college a cappella group. Neither of his parents did sports, but at least he could geek out over science with his mom. If he took Music Appreciation, he'd have something more to talk about with his dad too. In the end, Ms. Greene made the decision when he was signing up for classes after his tour of the school earlier that summer. "If I may," said Ms. Greene, sitting up straighter in her chair, "I think we should let Spencer sign up for the music elective. Physics can wait until next year. Here at Oakley we encourage expanding the mind through academic exploration." She sounded like she was quoting one of the motivational phrases plastered around the walls of her office.

No such posters lined the walls of the music room. Instead, there were the typical pictures of musical notes, plus black-and-white photos of musicians. Some Spencer recognized from Dad's record collection—Mahalia Jackson, Duke Ellington—and others he didn't know.

Spencer picked his seat and watched the rest of the students trickle in after the warning bell rang. A few of them looked familiar, but they didn't acknowledge him. Good, at least he was flying under the radar. A few seconds later, the teacher walked in. Her dress, made out of yellow kente cloth, fanned out around her. Spencer hadn't thought it was possible for a teacher to be cool, but there was no other word for it. She looked like she had just got back from vacation in Wakanda.

"Good afternoon, everyone. I'm Ms. Hart. Welcome to Music Appreciation." Her smile seemed to light up every corner of the drab room. She started with roll call and then launched into an explanation of the syllabus.

She was just going over the part about how while this class may be an elective, she still expected everyone to take it seriously and anybody who was anticipating an easy grade could leave right now, when the door opened and Justice Cortes, the dirt bike riding, soccer playing, Wesley Crusher look-alike, strolled in.

Spencer's heart fluttered like hummingbird wings in his chest. He'd been low-key disappointed that he hadn't had any classes with Justice, until he remembered his disastrous attempts at conversation that morning.

Considering Ms. Hart's lecture at the beginning of class, Spencer braced himself for her reaction to Justice's tardiness.

Justice aimed his crooked grin at Ms. Hart. "Did you miss me?"

Ms. Hart opened her arms. "Come give me a hug." She wrapped her arms around him and rocked him side to side the same way that Spencer's aunt hugged him whenever they visited her in New York.

"Sorry I'm late. I was talking to Coach about something."

"It's okay. Find a seat."

As if Spencer's thoughts were sending out a homing beacon, Justice looked over in his direction, making eye contact, and Spencer understood what Gimli saw when he gazed upon Galadriel. But, no. Just no. He hadn't even known this kid existed five hours ago. It was scientifically impossible to develop a crush in that amount of time, right? And, besides, he wasn't in the position to be crushing on anybody.

But of course, Justice chose the empty seat right next to him. For the next ten minutes Spencer tried very hard to concentrate on what Ms. Hart was saying, but it was difficult because his leg kept brushing against Justice's in the small circle.

Finally, Ms. Hart put down the syllabus in her hand and said, "Okay, everybody up. I know it's almost time to go home. Let's shake off this afternoon sluggishness."

She then led them through a series of stretches. Spencer became very aware of every sound that Justice made next to him as he stretched, and had to remind himself to look at Ms. Hart and not at Justice when she demonstrated a weird hip-swiveling routine.

Spencer was relieved when they finally finished and he could retreat to the safety of his seat, but Ms. Hart had other ideas. "Now, just because this isn't choir, doesn't mean I'm not going to make you sing."

Maybe he should've taken physics after all. Spencer had never been good at singing, but his voice had become much more unpredictable lately even when he was only talking.

Ms. Hart moved to the piano and played a scale. "We're going to do sirens. Start on the low note and I want you to slide up to the high note and back down again." She demonstrated the exercise, her voice rich and melodic. "Got it?"

She cued them in and Spencer opened his mouth to sing. He hit the low note all right, but then his voice cracked, sounding like a tortured goat. He saw the corners of Justice's mouth turn up. The tips of Spencer's ears went red and he switched to mouthing for the rest of the exercise.

When the torment was finally over and they were allowed to sit down again, Ms. Hart addressed the class. "This semester we're going to be exploring different music genres. Where there are people, there is music. I'm sure you all listen to music all the time. Like right now. Cole, I can see the AirPod in your ear."

Cole, a white kid with a buzz cut, sheepishly removed the AirPod.

"But who can tell me, what is music?" asked Ms. Hart.

The class shifted uneasily.

When nobody answered she said, "Come on, folks, this isn't a trick question."

A girl raised her hand. "It's like organized noise."

"Organized noise. Nice. What else?"

A few more kids raised their hands and she called on them.

Spencer opened his notebook to start writing down notes, but jumped when Justice's voice whispered in his ear.

"I heard you're trying out for the soccer team."

A shiver ran down Spencer's spine. He shrugged. He didn't trust his voice enough to speak.

"Are you any good?"

Spencer kept his eyes on Ms. Hart, not wanting to look at Justice. "I guess," he whispered back. He'd led his old team to championship victory in middle school, but he couldn't tell Justice that since it was a girls' team.

"Coach seems to think you are, anyway," continued Justice. "And Macintosh was practically skipping when he told me what happened in PE." He chuckled softly, shaking his head. "I've never seen anyone so happy to be belted with a ball before. But a word of advice: This isn't like playing in the backyard with your little brother. We're ranked second in the league. You'll need to be able to keep up."

Spencer bristled at that. "What makes you think I can't keep up?" The words left his mouth too loudly, causing Ms. Hart to pause and look over in their direction. But seriously, who did this kid think he was? He'd never even seen Spencer play.

Justice waited until Ms. Hart went back to her lesson to answer. "No offense, but you're like half the size of everyone else on the team. Not to mention the rest of the league. Look, come to tryouts if you want, but I just don't want you to get your hopes up."

Spencer opened his mouth to tell Justice where he could shove his hopes, but Justice was looking intently at Ms. Hart as if the conversation had never happened. Still disgruntled, Spencer attempted to do the same.

"Music can be found in every country," Ms. Hart was saying. "In every culture, and across every time period. Who can tell me where music began?"

Justice raised his hand so fast that it created a breeze that ruffled Spencer's hair. Ms. Hart called on him. Spencer expected him to say Nashville because of his country twang, but to his surprise he said, "Africa."

Ms. Hart smiled, her teeth flashing white against her dark skin. "That's right. Every genre can be traced back to its African roots. This semester, we're going to study how music has evolved over time. For your final project, you'll choose a song that has been covered by multiple artists across genres and identify how the different interpretations affect its message. I'll give you more information about that later on in the year. Now, I know it's been a long day. Let's finish up by listening to some music." She put on old-school R&B similar to what Spencer's dad jammed to when cleaning the house.

Spencer crossed his arms and tried to let the music wash over him, but his mind kept wandering back to Justice's comment. The more he thought about it, the more annoyed he got. Who was Justice to tell him what he could and could not do? Though trying out for the team didn't exactly mesh with keeping his head down, he sure as hell wasn't going to let Justice have the final word.

The fridge cast a blue glow as Spencer chugged orange juice straight from the carton later that evening. He peered through the doorway to the dining room, where Dad graded papers and Mom was setting the table for dinner.

"Cliff, can you move your stuff, we'll be eating soon. Spencer!" she called.

Spencer swallowed his mouthful. "I'm right here."

Mom looked into the kitchen and wrinkled her nose. "Use a glass, Spence. And close the fridge door. You weren't raised in a barn."

Spencer let out an *oink* before closing the fridge like she'd asked. He left the kitchen and snuck up behind Dad, throwing his arms around his neck.

"Look who finally decided to leave his room," Dad said as he wriggled out of Spencer's grasp.

"I was recharging."

"Connie, did you forget to plug him in last night?"

Spencer rolled his eyes. Being an introverted child of two extroverts was exhausting.

He took a seat at the table next to Dad. "Are we waiting for Theo?"

"Let's go ahead and get started," said Mom. "He needed a little chill-out time after school. He'll come when he's ready." She piled some chili on his plate. "So, tell us more about your day, you hardly said anything on the ride home." She kept her tone light, but a slight waver to her voice betrayed her nerves. When she'd picked him up after school, Spencer had kept to mostly monosyllable responses, too drained for anything else.

Spencer shrugged. "It was all right."

"Thank you for that description, Mr. Shakespeare," said Dad. "It's like I was actually there." He turned to Mom. "We're paying how much to send him to that place, and he can barely string a sentence together. Shaking my head."

Spencer rolled his eyes again. His parents had done their best to hide negative reactions to his transition, but he'd heard enough to know that some people called them abusive for supporting him. He wished he could tell them that the only abuse he suffered was his dad's corny jokes.

"Dad, first of all, it's SMH. Second, you only write it online. Third, nobody really uses it anymore."

"Thank you for that enlightening lecture, Professor

Harris. It's not like I have a PhD or anything," he added under his breath in a mock whisper.

"Call me Spencer. Professor Harris is my father."

Dad tossed his crumpled napkin at him and attempted to put him in a headlock.

"Cliff, please unhand our child." Mom sighed dramatically and turned back to Spencer. "Did you meet anybody nice?" Spencer noticed that she had barely touched her chili.

Spencer hastily shoveled another spoonful in his mouth to avoid answering, burning his tongue in the process. Just then, Theo entered the dining room wearing nothing but socks and underwear with blue manatees on them.

"Hey sweetie, we wear pants at the table, remember?" said Mom.

Theo looked down. "Oh yeah." He ran back out of the room.

"What about Theo?" asked Spencer, thankful for the distraction of his younger brother. "How was his first day?"

Mom and Dad exchanged a glance. Mom lowered her voice. "He had a little trouble getting on the bus this morning after we dropped you off, so I had to drive him. And his teacher called; they want to set up a meeting this week. I just hope we made the right decision moving him."

Dad reached over and squeezed Mom's hand.

"There's always tomorrow, right?" said Spencer.

"Right," said Mom. "Oh! Tell Dad about that boy from this morning. Do you have any classes with him?"

Spencer's fork missed his mouth. "Yeah, one." He leaned down to pick up a bean that had fallen on the floor before his tabby cat, Luna, could eat it. If the table hid the pink blush spreading across his cheeks, that was only a bonus.

"What's his name?"

Spencer sensed an incoming rapid-fire round of questioning. Mom used to be an ER nurse and was a pro at weaseling out information from mortified patients about what they were trying to stick where. It was only a matter of time before she cracked him.

"Justice." Justice, who didn't think he could hack it on the soccer team, he thought bitterly. Which reminded him . . . "He's on the soccer team. I also met the coach, who said I should come to tryouts." His voice went up at the end, turning it into a question.

Mom choked on her water. "The boys' team?"

"Well, yeah." What other team would he mean? "I've got the permission slip here." He took the form out of his pocket and handed it to Mom.

Mom scanned the form. Then his parents had a wordless conversation that involved lots of raised eyebrows and pursed lips. Mom broke the silence. "We don't think that's the best idea."

"Why not?" said Spencer, raising his voice.

"The plan was that you were going to ease into this transition," she said. "Let's not complicate things. Think about it: Where would you shower? And what about overnights?

There might be hazing rituals that involve nudity. There's a boatload of things that could go wrong. We don't want to go through what happened before."

Of course, Spencer had similar concerns. But it was *his* life and it should be *his* decision. "But this morning you were going on about how I needed to make friends."

"Yes, but there are other ways to make friends. I'm sure there are other activities you can join that maybe aren't as physical."

And there it was: She didn't think he could handle playing with the boys' team. He waited for Dad to step in to back him up, but he was adding spoonful after spoonful of sour cream to his chili, and not looking at him.

Mom continued, "What about AV club? You used to love making those little movies with Theo."

"Yeah, like a million years ago."

"Let's make a deal. This semester you join AV club, then Dad and I will think about soccer for next year." Mom folded the permission form and put it in her pocket. Conversation ended.

Spencer stabbed a bean with his fork. His parents might support his transition, but they would never truly see him as a boy.

After dinner Spencer went into his bedroom, shut the door against the world, and sank into his beanbag chair. He groaned when he heard Luna scratching at the door outside. He got up and opened the door for her. She leaped onto his bed and began kneading his blankets, purring. He nuzzled his face against her fur, then picked up his phone and called Aiden. He'd know what to do.

"So, how was it?" Aiden picked up after the first ring, and his familiar, raspy voice formed a warm cocoon around Spencer. It was wild to think he'd only known him since June. At trans camp they'd discovered that they only lived about thirty minutes away from each other and Aiden had invited Spencer to a local trans support group, which met every month.

"Not too bad, I guess."

"Dude, seriously? Has anyone told you that you're kind of hard to read? Don't make me claw it out of you."

"It was okay. Oh, I met one of your fans."

"Are we talking YouTube, music, or memes?" Spencer could practically hear Aiden grinning through the phone.

"Is the zine still not taking off the training wheels?"

"You could say that. I get that they hired me as the Gen Z whisperer, but I want to be able to write a story that matters, not recycle Twitter posts and TikToks. Anyway, back to my number one fan."

Spencer groaned good-naturedly. If it were anyone else, he'd be annoyed at the arrogance. Luckily Aiden's heart was twice as big as his head.

"Their name is Riley. They listen to your music. I . . . might have said you could hook us up with tickets."

"Trying to shoot your shot, huh?"

Spencer gave a slight shrug. "No, Riley's nice, but not my type."

"What *is* your type?" It wasn't the first time Aiden had asked him that. He was always suggesting people Spencer might be interested in, but Spencer had a hard enough time learning to love and accept his own body, let alone inviting someone else to.

Justice's face came unwillingly to mind. Spencer shook his head to clear it.

"I don't want to talk about my love life or inflate your already humongous ego. I need your advice." Spencer explained the situation about soccer tryouts and his parents not letting him go.

"I know what you want me to say. You want me to tell you that you should disobey your parents and go to prove to them that a trans guy can keep up with a bunch of cis boys. That way, when they find out, which they will because no offense, dude, you've got all the stealth of a drunk rhinoceros, you won't feel as guilty because I gave you permission."

That was what Spencer liked most about Aiden, he kept him honest.

"So I shouldn't go to tryouts?"

"I didn't say that. But *you* need to make the decision. Not me. You're not roping me into this one. Your mom already thinks I'm the anti-Christ."

"That's not true. Number one, my mom's an atheist and I'm pretty sure you need to believe in Christ to believe in an anti-Christ."

"Interesting theory. Not sure if it holds up. Look, I have to finish a post for tomorrow. Just do what you think is best. I'll see you on Saturday, right?"

On Saturday there was a barbecue for the trans support group they went to. "Yeah, I'll be there. Thanks Aiden. I think I'm going to do it."

"Good luck, bro. Love you, bye," said Aiden.

Spencer settled back on his beanbag and turned on FIFA. He controlled his favorite soccer player, Rafi Sisa, on the screen. If Sisa, the son of a dirt farmer who grew up playing barefoot in Ecuador, could become a professional soccer player, then he sure as hell could try out for a high school team.

Four

The only sound in the car the next morning was Theo reciting the narration to the show on his tablet seconds before the narrator said it. When they finally reached Oakley, Spencer opened the door and got out without a word.

Mom rolled down her window. "I'll pick you up after AV club. Have a good day, sweetie."

Thanks, but I've got other plans, he thought. Plans that didn't include AV club. He held tight to his backpack where he had hidden his boots last night. His PE kit would have to do for clothes.

They were playing basketball in PE, which wasn't Spencer's favorite sport on the best of days. It didn't help that he spent the whole period second-guessing his decision.

He jumped when Coach Schilling pulled him aside after class and said, "Ready for tryouts, Harris?" It looked like he had actually brushed his hair that morning and put on better-fitting, less grungy sweatpants. He was still wearing the hoodigan.

"Yeah, I'll be there."

"Good man," said Coach. He clapped a hand on Spencer's shoulder. "See you after school."

At lunchtime, the smell of burnt fish sticks and tater tots turned Spencer's stomach. Or maybe it was just nerves as he searched for a place to sit and eat his lunch in the crowded cafeteria.

He found an empty seat at the end of a table and opened his lunch, trying not to feel too sorry for himself, eating alone in a cafeteria full of people. His eyes settled on a long rectangular table where Justice, Macintosh, and a half dozen other boys sat. If everything went to plan that afternoon, soon he'd be sitting there too.

With lunch over, he counted down the seconds until the end of the day. When the last bell finally rang, he decided to change in a bathroom stall instead of the locker room with the rest of the people trying out.

By the time he made it outside, several boys were already there, passing the ball around the soccer pitch. He spotted Justice laughing after he nutmegged another player, sending the ball between his legs, sprinting behind him and picking the ball up again before the player even knew what happened.

He sat in the grass and pulled on his old boots. He hadn't

worn them for at least a year and they pinched his toes. He hoped he had enough money saved to get new ones. Then a whistle blew from the pitch and he stood, wiping his sweaty palms on his shorts.

He was usually a good kid. He didn't have much choice. When Theo turned two, it became obvious that he was different—not bad, just different. At first, Spencer didn't understand why Theo would have meltdowns if his peas touched his chicken nuggets, or when the seam in his socks rubbed his toes the wrong way. At his preschool open house, while the other toddlers sang a song, Theo stood on the bleachers with his eyes squeezed shut and his hands clasped tight over his ears.

After that, his parents were so busy getting Theo tested, driving him to his speech pathologist, working with his occupational therapist, that Spencer was often left alone to do his own thing. With Theo, there was always something to worry about, so it fell to Spencer to make life easier for his parents. He didn't want them to have to worry about two kids. Sure, sometimes his parents missed his games, and during his middle school graduation, Dad had to take a screaming Theo out of the auditorium before his name was called, but that didn't bother Spencer. Too much. But when Spencer did screw up—maybe he forgot to do his homework, or talked back to a teacher—he could count on Theo doing something that would make his errors pale in comparison.

But if he did this, and he wanted to, there was absolutely nothing Theo could do that would erase the fact that he deliberately disobeyed his parents. He'd have to be careful, he couldn't get caught, and if he did, he had to make sure he had something to show for it: proof he could make the team.

After a brief introduction and drills, Coach Schilling split them up into two teams to play a scrimmage, which disintegrated into complete chaos seconds after he blew his whistle with everyone playing like fourteen teams of one.

Spencer soon found himself lost in a crush of players all fighting for the ball. The one time he did manage to get a touch, he was steamrollered by Travis, a human brick wall. He lay on the ground, thinking it would be more convenient to stay put.

Coach Schilling's voice boomed from the sidelines. "For heaven's sake, you're on the same team. Save that aggression for a real game."

Travis helped Spencer to his feet. "Sorry, are you okay?" His voice was surprisingly gentle.

"Yeah, I'm fine."

Travis brushed grass clippings off his shoulder. Spencer's knees buckled. The kid really didn't know his own strength.

"Thirty-second water break," said Coach Schilling. His hair stood up in tufts from where he pulled it in frustration.

Spencer got his bottle from his backpack and sprayed water into his mouth and assessed his performance. It was amazing how quickly his body had remembered how to play. He'd done well during the drills, but he needed to step it up in the scrimmage if he had any chance at making the team. Justice came up alongside him and grabbed his own water bottle from the bench.

"I did try to warn you," he said.

"What are you talking about?" asked Spencer.

"You're being crushed out there. I can see it. Coach can see it. No shame in quitting."

Spencer stuffed his water bottle back into his backpack. "Screw you." He walked back onto the pitch with renewed vigor.

The scrimmage had taught him two things: One, he wasn't the strongest or the fastest, but what Spencer could do was find open places that the other players didn't see. Two, Justice underestimated him, which meant the others likely did too. He needed to use that to his advantage. Plus, with his small frame, he would probably be left unguarded most of the time anyway. So, when the game started up again, instead of getting crushed in the scuffle, Spencer paced around the field scanning for opportunities. His moment came when one of the players on the other team lost the ball and it whizzed past him. Spencer intercepted it and took off running toward the goal. He showed off his footwork, stepping over the ball to keep it from his opponents.

Once he was in shooting range of goal, he looked up to see Cory, a tall, gangly Asian kid who was trying out for goalie, trembling between the posts. He reminded Spencer of a baby giraffe: leggy with no coordination. Spencer could take him. He dribbled forward, feinting right, then left, daring Cory to come off his line. When Cory moved forward, Spencer curled the ball across the goal to Micah, a Black boy who was a striker, meters away from an open goal.

Micah drew back his foot and kicked the ball. It whooshed through the air and slammed into the goalpost.

"God bless it, Jenkins," yelled Coach Schilling. "How could you miss that?"

Spencer understood Coach's frustration, even if he didn't understand his method of swearing. By Spencer's count, they had a defender who couldn't defend without fouling, and a striker who couldn't hit a target three feet in front of him. What next? A goalie who couldn't save?

The ball rebounded in Justice's direction. He controlled the ball, then glanced around to see who he could pass it to.

"I'm open!" called Spencer.

He read the conflict in Justice's face. Justice hesitated, then flicked it to Spencer. It stuck to Spencer's feet like Velcro. He locked eyes with Cory. But it wasn't the face of a scared boy looking back. Instead, he saw his parents telling him he couldn't play boys' soccer. He saw Justice telling him he should quit. And he saw Coach in the team photograph last year, looking hollow in defeat, and the knowledge that he, Spencer, could be the missing puzzle piece to winning the League Cup.

Spencer feinted left this time, then right, and smashed the ball into the back of the net.

After changing back into his regular clothes, Spencer splashed water on his face and doused himself in Axe. Still flushed from the exertion, he headed up to the grassy hill by the drop-off/pickup area to wait for Mom.

His legs shook like jelly, but his body felt purified, like he'd sweated out all the stress and anxiety from the last couple days. His head was clearer than it had been in months. This sense of calm was one of the things he loved most about soccer.

He took out his phone and saw he had a text from Aiden wishing him luck at tryouts. As he began typing a reply, he heard voices come from the direction of the parking lot below. He recognized one of them as Macintosh's.

"What do you think about the new talent?"

"The goalie needs work." That was Justice.

Spencer ducked lower so they wouldn't see him if they happened to look up.

"He has potential. I can work with him," said Macintosh. "Forwards?"

"Micah's foot is a rocket but he needs to improve his aim."

"Agreed. Midfield?"

There was a pause. "The twins were good," said Justice, referring to a pair of identical twins named Zac and Wyatt.

"And Spencer?"

Another pause. Spencer held his breath. "I know you like him, but I have to be honest, I don't see it."

Spencer released his breath. He'd suspected that Justice didn't like him for whatever reason, but hearing it confirmed out loud hurt more than he thought it would.

"Why not? Did you see that pass to Micah? He reminds me of—"

"Don't say Nate. He doesn't belong in the same sentence as Nate, let alone the same team. He's not at our level."

Spencer couldn't hear Macintosh's response over the angry pounding of blood rushing through his ears. He took several deep breaths to calm down as he watched them leave, Macintosh in his Jeep and Justice on his bike. He was still seething when Mom's car pulled up to the school. He stood, brushing grass off his pants.

"Hey sweetie, been waiting long?" she asked when he climbed in.

"Not really."

She sniffed the air and wrinkled her nose. "Why do you smell like a middle school dance? Did you try to drown yourself in body spray?"

Spencer made a mental note not to use enough Axe to blast a hole in the ozone layer next time.

"Can I see the AV room?" interjected Theo.

"Um, maybe later," said Spencer, thankful he couldn't see Theo's face in the back seat. Lying to Theo felt ten times worse than lying to his parents.

"How was AV club?" asked Mom.

"It was fun."

She opened her mouth to ask another question but Spencer cut her off before she could dig deeper and uncover the truth. "Mom, I'm tired. Can we talk about it later?"

She frowned slightly, but said, "Of course, sweetie. I'm sure you had a long day."

Spencer stretched out on a towel soaking in the late summer sun. The smell of hot dogs filled the air, along with the sound of children shrieking and the sizzle of burgers on a grill.

It was Saturday afternoon and he was at an end-of-summer barbecue for Family and Friends of Transgender Kids and Teens of Northeast Ohio. He couldn't think of a better way to recover after surviving his first week at Oakley. He allowed himself to relax after being on constant alert for days. It hadn't helped that he'd been having trouble sleeping since tryouts. Coach Schilling said he'd be posting decisions soon, but Spencer had checked the bulletin board outside the locker room every morning since, and hadn't seen a thing.

Beside him, Aiden groaned. Spencer cracked open an eye to look at him. "What?"

Aiden tossed his phone on the towel. "It's my boss."

"You want to talk about it?"

"Nah, it's boring. Just another pitch shot down."

Aiden looked disappointed. His black-dyed hair and snakebite piercing might make him appear intimidating, but Spencer knew he was a softy, even if Mom still eyed him suspiciously sometimes.

"What was your friend's name? The one who likes my band?" asked Aiden.

"Who? Riley? We're not really friends."

Aiden rolled over on his side to look at Spencer. "Have you thought about inviting them to our next meetup? It might be good for them to meet other trans kids."

Spencer bit his cheek. "No, I haven't exactly come out to them."

"Still want to be completely stealth, then?" Aiden nodded slowly.

"Yeah, I just feel like the fewer people who know, the better. The more people who know, the greater the risk of rejection."

"Or acceptance," Aiden said.

"What?" asked Spencer.

"You're always assuming the worst. Yeah, coming out could go badly, but maybe you'll find a new ally."

Spencer rolled a piece of grass between his fingers. It was different for Aiden. His moms were lesbians, so he'd been around queer spaces his whole life. "If you had the option of being stealth at school, would you take it?" asked Spencer.

Aiden turned on his back again and drummed his fingers against his chest before answering. "Honestly, no. Some people at school don't know I'm trans and it's not like I lead with it when I meet someone, but I don't mind being open about it. I think it's about what you're comfortable with. But listen, Riley probably feels pretty alone if they've only just come out."

"Mm." Spencer tossed the ball of grass away. He could invite Riley, but he wanted to keep those parts of his life separate. Besides, Riley's happiness wasn't his responsibility.

Spencer told himself all that, but he wasn't sure if he believed it.

On Monday morning, Spencer arrived at first period early. Coach had all weekend to make decisions. Surely, he'd announced the team by now. Spencer raced to the bulletin board, but there was nothing about tryout results. Feeling deflated, he went into the locker room and sat down heavily on a bench. But a moment later, Macintosh sidled up to him in only his boxer briefs and swatted him playfully with his shirt.

"You might want to check the bulletin board *after* class, Twinkle Toes." He winked.

Spencer spent the rest of the class buzzing with excitement. As soon as they were dismissed, he pushed his way through the throng of people in front of the bulletin board, his heart pounding as he got closer. He found the team list for boys' soccer and scanned for his name. There it was, written in black ink—*Spencer Harris.*

He felt a hand on his shoulder and turned around to see Coach Schilling grinning. "First practice is tomorrow. You and me, kid. This is our year."

Spencer's excitement carried him all the way through lunchtime, when he brought his tray of microwave-warmed spaghetti to the QSA meeting. After doing names and pronouns, Grayson took the floor.

"Okay, let's hear some ideas for what we can bring to the administration to make Oakley a better place for queer students. Last year, we petitioned for all-gender couples' tickets at school dances, which ended up being a huge success. What do you think we should do this year?"

Riley raised their hand tentatively. "What about gender-neutral bathrooms?"

"That's a nice idea," said Grayson, "but we're looking for something that will benefit more students. Like with the tickets, now friends can buy couples tickets, which are cheaper, and go together."

"What about cis kids who want privacy while using the bathroom," asked Riley.

"I'm just saying it would probably be pretty difficult to persuade the administration to go for it just because some people are pee shy," said Grayson. "Let's hear some other ideas."

Riley stuffed their hand back in the pocket of their hoodie. Spencer had a choice to make. Being an ally to Riley when nobody was around meant nothing if he wasn't willing to stand up for them publicly as well.

"So, we just shouldn't do it because it's hard?" asked Spencer, unable to keep the contempt from his voice.

Everybody turned to stare. He thought about backing down, but he was too far in. "I mean, yeah, dances are great, but peeing is kind of essential. And it's not just trans kids," he continued. "What about kids with disabilities?" he said, thinking of Theo.

"They've got accessible stalls," said Brianna, a girl with an undercut.

"But if their aide is a different gender, then they'd be able to help them out in the bathroom."

The room fell into a tense silence until Grayson said, "Good point, Spencer."

The conversation moved on, but Spencer could still sense eyes on him. He felt a little embarrassed, but also a little something like pride. Even if he wasn't out, he could still support his community.

After the meeting, Riley hung back until everyone had left.

"Thanks for sticking up for me," they said.

"No worries. They were being pretty crappy allies."

"Yeah, but sometimes I expect that from cis people. No offense," they added quickly.

Spencer glanced around the empty room. It was just the two of them. He could let Riley assume he was cis, or . . .

"None taken. I'm not exactly cis."

"Wait." Awareness dawned on Riley's face. "You're—"

"Yeah, but please don't tell anyone."

"Of course not."

Even though the more people who knew he was trans, the less likely it was he could stay stealth, he felt like he could trust Riley. He thought back to his conversation with Aiden. "I talked to Aiden. He said he'd try to get us tickets. Also, there's this meetup group we go to. I'll send you the info."

"That's awesome. Thanks, Spencer."

"Don't mention it."

He walked to his next class feeling lighter than he had in weeks.

Five

Spencer was brought back down to earth that evening when he realized that now that he had made the team, he had to find a way to get to practice without his parents knowing.

He tossed and turned in his bed trying to come up with a possible solution. There was always the AV club excuse, but at some point, he'd have to show Theo the equipment. Maybe he could say he was staying late for the QSA? But what would happen when he had an actual QSA event? His parents would probably get pretty suspicious if he was always doing something with them.

In the end, his restless night was all for nothing. At breakfast that morning, Spencer nearly dozed off into his bowl of cereal, but was jerked completely awake when Mom unzipped Theo's backpack and dumped out the contents. Pencils, rulers, and a fancy-looking calculator clattered onto the kitchen counter. Mom sighed. "Do you think you could ride your bike today? Dad and I have to meet with Theo's teacher after school."

"Is everything okay?" Spencer stifled a yawn.

Mom gestured at the pile. "Your brother's having a bit of a tough time. You know change is hard for him. He's still refusing to ride the bus and now he's having trouble adapting to all the rules at his new school. His teacher sent an email about stealing and I'm pretty sure *that*"—she pointed at the calculator—"doesn't belong to Theo. And you know how at Montessori they were allowed to use the bathroom whenever they wanted? Last week, Theo got in trouble for not asking to go to the bathroom, so then he thought that he was *never* allowed to go and he tried to hold it but had an accident in class yesterday. I'm sure everything will be fine, but—"

"I'll ride my bike," said Spencer, a little too eagerly. According to his calculations he'd have enough time to go to practice and be freshly showered and doing homework at the kitchen table by the time they got home. With the issue of going to the first practice solved, Spencer returned to his cereal with vigor.

Then he realized how messed up it was to be happy about Theo struggling, especially when it was his fault Theo had to switch schools in the first place. He dropped his spoon in the bowl, no longer hungry.

"Thanks for stepping up, Spence," said Mom, which made him feel even worse.

. . .

At 2:30, Spencer approached the door to the locker room. He could hear laughter and music coming from inside. It reminded him of his old team, where the locker room was a sacred place. Before games it was a tinderbox of tension and anticipation, and afterward a place of celebration or solace, depending on the outcome.

But now there were new customs and rituals to learn.

Spencer's hand shook as he twisted the handle and went in. Most of the team was already there. Cory, the gangly giraffe of a goalie, was watching a video on his phone, and the twin midfielders, Zac and Wyatt, were arguing over whose shoe was whose. Macintosh smiled at him as he entered.

"Twinkle Toes, good to have you on the team!"

Spencer cringed at the nickname, but at least Macintosh didn't seem too upset about the incident in PE.

As Spencer passed by, Justice made a show of shoving his duffel bag into a locker. He'd been quiet in Music Appreciation, which Spencer didn't mind one bit. He wasn't expecting Justice, who clearly thought he was God's gift to soccer, to congratulate him for making the team.

Spencer found a corner and quickly changed into his shorts, facing the row of lockers. After a week of furtively dressing for PE, Spencer realized that nobody was paying him any attention. Sure, some guys, like Macintosh, traipsed around in their boxer briefs, but more were huddled in their own corners, shooting nervous glances as they peeled off their clothes attempting to reveal as little as possible. It was almost like puberty sucked for everyone. Outside on the pitch, a beaming woman with a clipboard and an *I want to talk to your manager haircut* tracked him down. "You must be Spencer. I'm the team administrator and Daniel's mom. He told me all about you," she said.

"Daniel?" Spencer asked, confused.

"Daniel Macintosh. Now, I wanted to catch you before practice because it looks like we don't have a permission slip for you."

"Oh, right." In all his planning, he hadn't thought of that. He scratched the back of his neck, then gave her his most innocent smile. Time to put his baby face to good use. "Do you have any extras? I lost mine."

She narrowed her eyes suspiciously. "We're not supposed to let you play without one."

Spencer looked up at her from under his eyelashes.

"Oh, what the heck." She handed him another form. "Grab a pinnie and bring this back to Coach Schilling before next practice."

Spencer picked up a fluorescent numbered training bib from a cardboard box and thanked her. He'd figure out what to do with the form later.

"Try not to break anything," she called after him.

As he joined everyone else on the pitch, he felt like a

hobbit in the land of giants. He had to balance on his tiptoes to see over everyone's shoulders at Coach Schilling, who stood in the middle of the circle.

"If you're looking for a weekend leisure league, this isn't the right team for you. We practice three days a week and have games most Saturdays. We also compete for the Ohio Preparatory School Soccer League Cup, where we came in second last year." He spat on the ground like he'd tasted something unpleasant.

He paused for a moment, then rubbed his hands together energetically. "Now, you all should know Macintosh, your captain and goalie."

A smile split across Macintosh's face. "I really think this will be our year."

"With the talent we have on this team, so do I," said Coach.

"There's also your vice captain, Justice Cortes. Youngest vice captain in Oakley history, I might add," said Coach, thrusting his chest out with pride.

Spencer resisted the urge to roll his eyes. No wonder Justice had such a big head.

"Now, I looked at the strengths each of you bring to this team and I threw my original playbook out the window and spent all week designing an innovative training program. The cornerstone to our approach is going to be passing."

Spencer almost choked on his spit.

"Macintosh, do you want to take it away?"

Macintosh clapped his hands once. "All right, let's start with a warm-up. We're going to run around the field once."

Easy. Spencer could do that in no time. Then he noticed a slight quirk to Macintosh's lips.

"But, we're going to do it in pairs wearing these. . . ." Macintosh held up a scarf.

"What's the point of this?" asked Justice. "Shouldn't we be doing drills or something?" He kicked at the ground impatiently.

"It will teach you how to anticipate the movement of your teammate," said Coach. "If you're going to be able to make accurate passes, you need to trust that your teammate will be there to get it."

"Okay, forwards link up with another forward, midfielders find a midfielder, and so on," said Macintosh.

Spencer found himself partners with Dylan, a wiry white kid who looked like a ferret.

Macintosh weaved between them handing out the scarfs, but stopped when he got to the twins. "I think we should split up the dream team. You've got an unfair advantage."

"Just because we're twins doesn't mean that we spend all our time tied to each other," said one of them. Zac, Spencer thought.

"Still, I'd like to mix it up a little. Zac, you go with Dylan."

Spencer moved to go stand next to Wyatt, but Macintosh stopped him.

"Hang on, Twinkle Toes. I want you with Justice."

"Why?" they both said at the same time.

Macintosh just smiled mysteriously and finished reassigning the teams.

Justice came over to him with a grimace on his face.

"Howdy, partner," said Spencer, in an effort to break the ice. If they were going to play well together, they needed to learn how to get along. But Justice didn't laugh; he barely acknowledged Spencer's existence. So Spencer decided it was best not to say anything else.

"Okay, everyone ready?" asked Macintosh.

"Let's just get this over with," mumbled Justice under his breath. He bent down to tie their legs together at the ankle. Spencer felt a spark when Justice's fingers brushed against his calf.

"On your marks, get set, go!"

Spencer went one way, Justice went the other, and they didn't make it one step before collapsing in a pile of limbs.

Justice managed to extract himself from Spencer and sat up. "This isn't going to work. Your legs are too short."

"Maybe yours are too long," Spencer shot back.

Justice hauled himself up, then stuck a hand under Spencer's armpit. Spencer jerked away. He wasn't used to having someone so close to him. Justice shot him a confused look. "I'm just trying to help you up," he said.

"I don't need your help." Spencer pushed off the ground.

Even at his full height, Spencer's chin only just reached Justice's shoulder.

"Let's think through this logically," said Spencer.

"Seriously? It's a three-legged race. One foot in front of the other. My seven-year-old brother could do it."

"I thought this was a serious team, not backyard soccer," said Spencer. Justice's mouth tightened, accentuating his jawline.

A whistle blew, surprising them both. "Oh, I'm sorry. Am I interrupting your tea party?" Coach bellowed from the sidelines. "Let's see some hustle!"

Spencer looked around. All the other pairs were far ahead of them, already halfway done with the lap.

"Okay," said Justice. "Right foot first."

"Fine."

They both took a step with their right foot. Justice pulled Spencer's left foot with it and they fell again.

"What are you doing?" yelled Justice, slamming his fist on the grass.

"You said right foot first."

"I meant *my* right, your left."

Spencer threw his hands up. "Well, why didn't you say that?"

"I didn't think I had to." Justice scowled and Spencer wondered how he ever found him cute.

The rest of the team returned from their lap while he and Justice had barely moved five feet.

A shadow fell over them. Spencer looked up to see Coach Schilling glaring down. "You two need to get it together."

"Coach, you know that was a stupid exercise," said Justice. "Unless you plan on making us play tied up like that during a game."

Coach Schilling ignored him. "I'm giving you an assignment: I want you to spend time with each other outside of school and outside of practice. Get to know one another. I've been thinking about using the two of you as our main midfield partnership, but until you show me you can work together, I'll have to use someone else. And with the wonder twins over there"—he gestured over to where Zac and Wyatt were heading the ball to each other without missing a beat— "you've got some stiff competition."

The heel on Spencer's left foot was killing him by the time he got home after practice. He gingerly peeled back his sock to reveal a huge blister. *Shit.* If he was going to keep playing, his boots weren't going to cut it.

After showering, he fetched the first aid kit from the bathroom cabinet and sat on the toilet. Wincing, he dabbed at his raw skin with an antiseptic wipe.

Suddenly, the bathroom door opened and Theo barged in, making Spencer jump and knock the first aid kit off the sink edge. It exploded, littering the floor with Band-Aids and gauze pads. Spencer scrambled to shove everything back in the first aid kit. He hadn't heard Mom's car pull in while he'd been in the shower.

"Closed door means don't come in, remember?" he said to Theo, attempting to keep his voice steady and hoping Theo hadn't seen anything.

"But I have to go," Theo whined, hopping from foot to foot. "What happened?" He pointed at Spencer's heel.

"Nothing."

"But you're bleeding."

"Shh," Spencer hushed him. He knelt in front of Theo, putting his hands on his brother's shoulders. "I've taken care of it. I need you to promise me that you won't tell Mom and Dad. Okay?"

Theo furrowed his brow, but nodded.

Spencer left the bathroom, but after he closed the door he couldn't get Theo's face, pinched with worry, out of his head. Theo had enough to deal with. He shouldn't have to keep Spencer's secrets as well.

Six

By the middle of the week, Spencer couldn't bend his legs without his muscles screaming in protest. He had to be careful not to wince around his parents, especially Mom, gritting his teeth to bite back the pain.

But he loved the ache in his body as his muscle fibers knit themselves back together stronger than before. When he flexed, it reminded him that his body was constantly growing and changing, aided by the testosterone gel he smeared on his shoulders every morning. Apart from the physical changes, like a deeper voice, broader shoulders, and the need to shave every two to four weeks, he gained a sense of calm and balance that wasn't there before going on hormones.

That sense of calm was put to the test at lunchtime on Wednesday when Spencer walked into the cafeteria, prepared to sit with Riley or the other QSA kids, but saw Macintosh waving his arms at him, looking like one of those inflatable flailing dudes outside of car dealerships.

"Hey, Twinkle Toes, come sit with us!"

Spencer nearly tripped over his feet as he made the long

walk across the cafeteria to where the soccer team sat for the first time.

"You're really trying to make that stick," he said to Macintosh when he got to the table.

"Oh, it will," said Macintosh. It was difficult to be mad at him with his golden retriever–like expression.

"Whatever you say, Daniel," said Spencer.

All the chatter stopped and Spencer thought he may have made a mistake until Macintosh let out a bark of laughter. "Twinkle Toes has jokes!"

The chatter started up again and Spencer nibbled at his sandwich and let his teammates' conversation wash over him, not exactly sure where he fit in, but happy he was there all the same. When lunchtime ended, he threw away his trash and was about to leave when Justice grabbed his arm to stop him, before dropping it quickly.

"Meet me after school," said Justice.

Spencer's eyes narrowed. "Why?" Justice hadn't said one word to him since practice.

Annoyance flickered across Justice's face. "Coach wants us to hang out, remember?"

"What if I'm busy after school?" asked Spencer. His only plans included homework, a long soak in the tub, and playing FIFA, but Justice didn't need to know that.

"Too bad. I'm not going to let Coach bench me because of this. Today. After school. Tell your mom you'll be late." Justice pushed past Spencer and out of the cafeteria.

What a grade A asshole. But if Spencer had any chance at getting time on the pitch, he had to play the game off it as well.

Justice tapped his foot impatiently as Spencer packed up after Music Appreciation. Spencer purposefully took his time zipping up his backpack, enjoying the increasingly frustrated look on Justice's face.

He'd texted Mom after lunch telling her he had another AV club meeting and would be home late. Luckily he'd taken his bike to school since Theo still wasn't riding the bus.

"Come on. We can ditch our backpacks in the team room. I've got a key," said Justice.

Once their backpacks were stowed, Spencer followed Justice down the hallway toward the school entrance. "So, where are we going for our bonding session?" He practically had to jog to keep up with Justice's long strides.

Justice pinched the bridge of his nose with a pained expression. "Please don't call it that."

Spencer took a perverse sort of pleasure in seeing Justice annoyed. He decided to push it slightly further. "What should I call it? A bro date?"

Justice whirled around so fast that Spencer crashed into him. "Do you ever shut up? I can't believe I ever thought you were quiet."

Spencer looked down and bit his lip. "Sorry."

Justice ran a hand through his hair. "No, *I'm* sorry. I've had a long day and I don't really have time for this. But I shouldn't have taken it out on you."

For the first time since meeting him, Spencer felt like he was getting a peek of the Real Justice. "We can do a different day," suggested Spencer.

"I can't, I'm busy."

"Doing what?"

They had reached the courtyard separating the entrance from the parking lot, where milky sunlight shone through the trees and warmed Spencer's skin.

"On days I'm not at practice I've got Bible study and then I also volunteer at an after-school soccer club. That's where I should be now, but here we are."

"Let's go," said Spencer. "I mean, if that's where you're supposed to be. We can go now. Together."

Justice's face lit up. "Seriously? That would be awesome."

"Yeah, I'm sure we can find time to squeeze in some bonding. Right, bro?"

Justice shoved Spencer's shoulder lightly. "Don't make me regret this."

When they reached the parking lot, Spencer went to unlock his bike, but Justice called him back. "You can get on mine. It will be faster."

Spencer eyed the dirt bike nervously. He'd never ridden

on one before and he hated to imagine what would happen if he got hurt. Honestly, even if he survived, Mom would still kill him if she found out.

Justice must have seen his hesitation. "You've got your helmet, right? I promise I'll drive really carefully." He got on the bike.

After a second, Spencer climbed on behind. He'd just add it to his list of things to feel guilty about.

"You might want to hold on," Justice said over the roar of the engine.

The bike jerked forward and Spencer wrapped his arms around Justice's torso.

"Not that tight!"

Spencer relaxed his grip but could still feel the thudding of Justice's heart against his palms and wondered if Justice could feel his own heart marching in a similar beat against his back. He pressed himself closer against Justice.

After a few minutes they pulled into a parking lot next to a squat, white building with a tall spire.

Spencer reluctantly detached himself from Justice. The ride had seemed to go by too fast. "This is a church," he said, then immediately regretted stating the obvious. Even though it wasn't Sunday, there were a surprising amount of cars parked in the lot.

"Yeah, my church sponsors the soccer club. It's where I met Coach. You okay?" asked Justice.

Spencer tried to keep his face as neutral as possible. His family wasn't religious. A strict Methodist upbringing had turned Mom off of organized religion.

But Spencer wasn't there for God. He was there to play soccer. "Yeah, I'm fine. Let's go."

They entered the church and walked down a hallway, following the sound of children's shouts and laughter until they reached a large multipurpose room. A boy about Theo's age with chin-length blond hair barreled into Justice, hugging him.

When the boy let go, Justice looked at Spencer. "Steady, this is my friend Spencer. Spencer, this is my little brother, Steadfast."

The names: Steadfast and Justice; Justice's mention of Bible study; volunteering at the church. Spencer mulled it over in his mind and started to put it all together. Justice was religious, or at the very least came from a religious family. Which could mean nothing, or it could mean that he believed Spencer's existence was a sin. Aiden would chastise him for his doomsday thinking, but he had a right to be wary. Mom tried to hide it from him, but he knew her parents struggled with his transition. More than once he'd heard his grandma say "God doesn't make mistakes."

"Here." Justice shoved a mesh bag in his hand, interrupting his thoughts. "Can you set out cones to mark the sidelines and the goals?"

"Sure." Spencer worked around the room setting up the cones as a few more kids trickled in. When he'd finished, he scanned the room for Justice and spotted him by a plastic rack of soccer balls. He wasn't alone. He was talking to a girl who looked around their age. She was pretty, with brown hair that ran down her back and past the waist of the long khaki skirt she wore. Spencer wondered if she was Justice's girlfriend and his breath hitched at the thought.

"Cones are done," he said, walking up to them.

The girl turned to look at him, scanning his body up and down. Spencer felt his insides squirm as if he were a tardigrade under a microscope.

Justice made the introductions. "Spencer, Martha, Martha, Spencer. He goes to my school."

Spencer put out his hand and Martha shook it.

"Nice to meet you. Are you thinking about joining our church?"

"He's just helping out with soccer club today," Justice cut in before Spencer could answer.

"How generous. I'll set these out." She held up a Tupperware of orange slices. "Anyway, I'm glad you could make it today. Otherwise the littles would be running around like loons." Martha shot a final look at Spencer before squeezing Justice's forearm and heading over to the snack table.

"Her dad's the pastor," said Justice, after she left.

"Oh." The word came out darker than he was expecting,

but he was pleasantly surprised that there was no mention of her being Justice's girlfriend.

"Shall we start?"

"Let's do it."

Justice called for everyone's attention. It took several tries to wrangle them all together. Spencer helped break up an orange-throwing fight between a couple boys and Justice had to confiscate a soccer ball from Steadfast, who wouldn't stop kicking it against the wall. Eventually, they managed to round all the kids up and arrange them in a circle.

"Are you ready to play a game?" asked Justice.

The kids cheered and Spencer nearly did a double take. This was not the grim-faced Justice he knew from soccer practice.

"Before we start, who can tell me the rules?"

Little hands shot into the air and Justice pointed at a boy with a major cowlick.

"Practice good sportsmanship, honor God, and have fun!" Everyone, including Justice, joined in on the last rule. Spencer faked a cough to stop himself from laughing at the cheesiness.

"I don't want Luke on my team. He sucks," said a dour-faced boy with orange pulp in his hair.

"Hey, now, that's not how we talk about our friends," said Justice gently. It was such a different tone than Spencer was used to. "How about you say sorry to Luke."

The boy muttered a passable apology and Justice

continued. "I thought we'd try something new today. I've got my friend here and I think it might be fun if all of you were on a team against us. Sound good?"

The kids cheered in agreement.

"Okay, Steady, do you want to lead stretches?"

While the kids were watching Steadfast, Justice turned to Spencer, his face more animated than Spencer had ever seen it.

"How about it? Us against them. Think we can win?"

Spencer did a quick head count. There were about a dozen kids there.

"I think we can take them." He grinned back.

That game taught Spencer two things about Justice. First, his touch was exquisite. Spencer thought his own feet were like bubble gum, but Justice's were like superglue.

Spencer's volley soared high over the heads of the kids and landed right at Justice's feet. He effortlessly dribbled through the swarm to pass the ball back to Spencer, who was near the goal. Spencer was about to shoot when the dour-faced boy crashed into him and he skidded across the floor.

"Hey!" called Justice. He came over and helped Spencer up. His fingers were callused and rough against Spencer's palm. "That's a penalty to us. Do you want to take it?" asked Justice

Spencer rubbed his hip where it hit the floor. He didn't think he was seriously hurt, but it would leave a bruise. "No, you can go ahead. I'll take it easy." It wasn't worth risking an actual injury playing against elementary schoolers.

Justice placed the ball in front of the goal, which was guarded by a tiny girl with blond pigtails who was wearing a long-sleeved floral dress. Justice took a deep breath, then ran up to the ball.

The goal could have been in outer space, that's how big of a miss it was. Maybe he was trying to take it easy on the little girl, but something about the muscle ticking in Justice's jaw told Spencer that the miss hadn't been on purpose.

That was the second thing he learned: For all his talk about Spencer not being good enough, maybe Justice wasn't so perfect himself.

The sky began to darken on the ride back to school, and by the time they arrived, droplets of rain were falling from the sky and dotting the ground. Spencer climbed off of Justice's bike, wincing at his sore hip.

"You okay?" asked Justice.

Spencer grimaced. "I'll be fine. The kid who tackled me could be some serious competition for Travis, though."

"Sorry about that." Justice smiled ruefully.

"Don't be. I actually had fun."

"You don't need to sound so surprised," Justice said. But he looked pleased.

"And now Coach will get off our backs, right?" said Spencer.

"Right." Justice rubbed the back of his neck. "About Coach, maybe don't mention me missing that penalty?"

Spencer frowned. "Of course." Though he was curious how a player as good as Justice could miss against someone who was practically a toddler.

Justice sighed in relief. "Cool. Hey, if your leg is bothering you, you can wait here. I'll get our backpacks from the team room."

"Oh, thanks." Spencer wasn't sure what caused Justice's personality change, but he had to admit, he liked this new side of him.

Spencer went over to his bike and unlocked it. Thunder rumbled overhead, then headlights flashed, and Spencer recognized Mom's Subaru pulling up.

Mom rolled down her window.

"What are you doing here?" asked Spencer, panic rising.

"I called and texted you. I saw that it was going to storm, so I decided to pick you up from AV club. I brought Theo. He wanted to see the film equipment." Theo waved from the back seat.

Spencer thought quickly. "AV club was canceled today."

"Canceled? What have you been doing this whole time?"

"Here's your backpack," said Justice, coming up behind him.

"Ah, now I see." Mom nodded knowingly. "Hi there, I'm Connie."

"I think we've met." Justice flashed her his winning smile.

"Yeah, you almost ran him over," cut in Spencer. He attached his bike to the back of the car, wanting the conversation to be finished as quickly as possible.

"Were you two working on a project or something?" Spencer didn't want to think about the "or something" she was imagining.

"We were—" began Justice.

But Spencer cut him off. "Yeah, in the library. Can't use your phone in there or the librarians will shush you. That's why I didn't see your texts." *Stop talking, stop talking, stop talking.*

Spencer felt Justice's eyes digging into him, but he didn't say anything.

"Well, it's a shame we can't see the AV equipment. Maybe next time."

The rain pounded down heavier.

"Get in, Spence. We can give you a ride as well," she offered Justice.

"It's okay, I live nearby."

Spencer opened the door, but Justice tugged on his sleeve, stopping him. "Wait, can I get your number? In case I have a question about the project?" He shot Spencer a surprisingly devilish smile.

Spencer quickly punched his number into Justice's phone and got in the car.

"Don't say anything," he said between clenched teeth.

"I wasn't going to," said Mom. But Spencer could see her mile-wide grin out of the corner of his eye.

That evening while Spencer was wrestling one of his dirty socks away from Luna, he got a text. He admitted defeat and let Luna keep the sock to check his phone.

Justice: Please tell me there's not a project I should've been working on

Spencer's fingers hesitated over his phone screen. He figured he owed Justice an explanation for his weird behavior.

Spencer: My parents don't exactly know I'm on the team

Justice: Wow. Who knew that Twinkle Toes was a badass?

Who knew that Justice, the altar boy, swore?

Spencer: It's not funny

For some reason, texting with Justice was easier than talking face-to-face.

Spencer: If they found out I'd have to quit the team

Justice: Then don't let them find out

Spencer frowned in confusion. Just last week Justice hadn't even wanted him to go to tryouts.

Spencer: I thought you'd be happy if I quit

Justice: Why would you say that?

Spencer typed out a response, then deleted it, before changing his mind and retyping it. He hit send before he lost his nerve.

Spencer: I thought I wasn't at your level . . .

Spencer counted the seconds until Justice's response.

Justice: You heard that?

Spencer: I did

Justice: I'm sorry, that was a crappy thing to say.
I don't want to explain over text. Meet me in the
team room tomorrow before school?

Being with Justice that afternoon was like peering through a kaleidoscope, every time he looked a different version of him shifted into view, each more intriguing than the last. Spencer had to admit he was curious at what else he might discover if given the opportunity. He waited a moment before responding.

Spencer: Okay

Seven

The next morning at breakfast, the idea of seeing Justice again made Spencer feel like he was going to vibrate out of his skin. After his first few bites of cereal hit his stomach like lead, he gave up on eating and stirred it around the bowl until it grew soggy, keeping one eye on the kitchen clock.

When the clock hit 7:30, he leaped up from the counter.

"You've got thirty minutes. Why are you leaving so early?" asked Mom, who was finishing packing Theo's lunch.

Spencer emptied his bowl in the sink, then put it in the dishwasher. "I . . . I've got to finish the project I was working on."

"With Justice?"

"Uh, yeah."

Mom's lips formed a tight line. "Is there something you're not telling me?"

Spencer's palms slicked with sweat. "No, why would you say that?"

Mom cupped her hands over Theo's ears and lowered her voice. "If you and this boy are engaging in certain behaviors, we'll need to talk about protec—"

"Ew, Mom. No. We're just working on a project."

"Right, I know all about projects." She put air quotes around the word.

"I'm going to be late." Spencer stuck his helmet on his head and moved for the door.

"This conversation isn't over, mister," Mom called after him.

He could still feel his face burning when he got to school. The parking lot was nearly empty, but Spencer saw Justice's bike. He locked his own, then went inside. His footsteps echoed in the deserted hallway, breaking up the eerie silence as he walked to the team room. He reached the athletics hallway and there was Justice wearing a heather-gray T-shirt and dark jeans. Justice's face broke into a smile when he saw Spencer, who immediately forgot how to walk on solid ground.

"Hey," he said, trying to sound casual, but failing when his voice cracked.

To his credit, Justice turned away to hide his smile. He unlocked the door to the team room, holding it open for Spencer.

The team room consisted of a long rectangular table in the middle with a dozen or so chairs around it. A large screen hung on the wall at one end, and there was a projector installed on the ceiling.

Spencer settled into one of the chairs, spinning it side to side while Justice powered on the projector and connected it to a laptop before taking a seat next to him. They were so close together that the hairs on Justice's arm grazed his own.

Justice still hadn't spoken and Spencer felt an overwhelming pressure to say something, anything, to fill the silence.

"You should've told me you were taking me to a movie. I would've brought popcorn." Maybe anything but that.

"I'm not taking you anywhere. And this isn't a date," said Justice, shifting next to him, creating more distance.

"I know. I was joking," muttered Spencer. And he was. Really. Spencer crossed his arms defensively. There would be no accidental hand brushing on his watch. "What are we doing here, anyway?"

"I want to show you something." Justice pressed play on the video. "This is from last year's final against Harlow. It came down to penalties."

Spencer watched as the Harlow and Oakley players rotated taking penalties. They were well matched. Justice was the last player to take the penalty for Oakley. If he missed, Harlow would win the game. Justice approached the penalty spot, did a stuttering run up, and missed the net completely, like he had last night.

Next to Spencer, Justice paused the video while onscreen Justice crouched and buried his face in his hands.

"Okay, that stinks, but it doesn't explain why you were a dick to me."

Justice let out a sigh. "I shouldn't have said what I said about you not being good enough for the team, because you are. You're, like, really good, Spence."

Spencer was immensely glad that the room was dark and Justice couldn't see him blushing. "You called me Spence."

Justice's brow furrowed. "Is that okay? I mean, I assumed people called you that."

"Yeah, it's fine. My family calls me that." Spencer cleared his throat. "Sorry, I'm still confused why you showed me that video and what it has to do with all this." He gestured vaguely around the room.

Justice angled his body toward Spencer's. "I had some personal things going on around last year's final and that missed penalty was the result. So I refocused and spent the rest of the year analyzing footage and coming up with a game plan with Coach and Macintosh for this year. But then when you came along, Coach threw that playbook out the window."

"You couldn't have explained that in a text? 'Hey Spencer, sorry I'm a jerk, but I have performance issues and took it out on you.'"

Justice chuckled softly. "Okay, I deserve that. And yeah, I

probably could've texted you, but that isn't the only reason I brought you here. Yesterday at soccer club, I got an idea." He navigated to another video. "This is the Fenton Foxes, the team we'll be playing at sectionals on the weekend."

The screen showed opponents taking free kick after free kick against the Foxes. The Fox players lined up in a wall to guard against the free kick. Sometimes the players in the wall jumped and sometimes they didn't.

"Can you tell when they're going to jump?" asked Justice.

Spencer leaned forward scrutinizing the footage, searching for a pattern, but there was none. Sometimes they jumped, sometimes they didn't. No matter which side of the pitch the kick was taken from, or who was in the wall, or the team they were playing against.

"I'll give you a hint. It wasn't me who figured this out, it was Macintosh. Who controls the box?" Justice restarted the video. This time, Spencer focused on the goalie. Every time the wall jumped, it was after the goalie had put up three fingers.

"The goalie?"

"Yeah."

"Why are you showing me this?"

"You know why we dominated yesterday?"

"Because we were playing against second graders?"

Justice shot him an annoyed look. "Well, yeah, but it helped that we could see over them." Justice pulled out a piece of paper and began scribbling. "Picture this: It's eighty-nine minutes into the game and we're tied. Micah gets fouled just outside the box and wins us a free kick, which I take. Where are you?"

"I dunno, around the box waiting to get the rebound when you miss."

"Wrong. You're in the wall. I know most teams stack the wall with taller players, but if we get a free kick, I need you to be in there. That way I can see over your head at the goalie. He'll give the signal. If the signal is to jump, I'll roll it under. Easy goal." His face grew more animated as he talked and Spencer could see just how much he cared about soccer. But he wasn't going to let him off that easy.

Spencer twisted his face as if deep in thought. "So, what you're saying is that you made me get up early and come here to tell me that you only want me on the team because I'm short?"

Justice buried his face in his hands. "No! What I'm saying is that I think you're really talented and the team needs you, Coach needs you, I need you. And I'm sorry for being a jerk. Do you forgive me?"

Spencer put his finger on his chin. "I'll forgive you on one condition."

"What's that?"

"You stop Macintosh calling me Twinkle Toes."

"Ah," said Justice with mock sadness. "That's one promise I'm afraid I can't make."

. . .

Spencer joined the team in a lineup at practice that afternoon and once again became aware of how small he was compared to everyone else. Not that soccer players needed to be super tall—hell, his favorite soccer player, Rafi Sisa, barely hit five-four—but it would be nice if he would hit his growth spurt. His endocrinologist reassured him it was coming, but it was sure taking its sweet time.

Coach Schilling stood in front of the team. "Four days. That's how long we've got until our first tournament game. We lose, we're out, and none of us want that. Now, you're all fine players, you wouldn't be here otherwise, but I need to see who the strongest eleven are. Today we're going to play a scrimmage to help me decide."

Spencer pulled himself up straighter. This was it, his chance to prove what he could do. He wasn't going through all this trouble of lying to his parents so that he could sit on the bench the whole season.

Coach Schilling continued, "Justice and Macintosh, you'll each be team captains for this scrimmage. Who calls heads?"

"I call heads," said Justice. Coach tossed the coin in the air. It landed George Washington side up. "Heads it is. Your pick, Justice."

Spencer crossed his fingers behind his back, praying that he wouldn't be picked last. Justice scanned the team, eyes landing on Spencer. He pointed at him. "Spencer, you're with me."

"Glad to see you two getting along," said Coach.

Spencer went to stand beside Justice while Macintosh made his first choice.

"Who should we pick?" Justice's breath tickled Spencer's ear. Cory, the gangly goalie, looked as nervous as Spencer had felt. He was the only other goalie on the team, so it was pretty obvious where he'd go, but Spencer thought it would be nice to put him out of his misery.

"Cory," he whispered.

Justice arched an eyebrow at him, like "seriously?" Spencer shot him a look like "yeah, don't be such an asshole."

Justice bit back a grin, shaking his head. "Fine, come on, Cory."

Cory did a subtle fist pump and joined them.

Once the teams were chosen, Spencer took his place in the left midfield. With three midfielders on their team, they decided on a 2-3-2 formation: Travis and Cameron playing defense; Spencer, Oscar, and Wyatt, one of the identical twins, in midfield; and Justice joining Micah as a forward. Macintosh arranged his team in a 3-2-2 formation.

Coach Schilling called out from the sidelines, "The Foxes are a defensive-minded team. They're going to make it hard to penetrate their line. It's important that your passing is fast and crisp, so we're going to play a game of two-touch soccer. Take one touch to control the ball and one touch to pass it. No more, no less. Use what we've been practicing."

Spencer squinted across the field to where Justice stood in the center for kickoff. Coach blew his whistle.

Justice passed the ball to Micah, whose powerful shot had the potential to burn a hole through the back of the net but only when he could find it. Spencer was open and called out for the ball, but Micah's pass sailed over his head and into the parking lot. There was a crash and a car alarm sounded.

Micah raised his hand in apology. "My bad."

The game started up again with Zac, the other midfield twin, on the ball for Macintosh's team. Travis tackled him from behind, spinning the ball across the field into open space. They collapsed in a tangle of legs.

"Travis, I appreciate the enthusiasm, but that's a surefire way to get sent off," called Coach Schilling, but he allowed play to continue.

Spencer avoided making direct challenges. Instead, he waited for the ball to spin out of control, then pounced, sprinting forward with it glued to his feet. He looked up to see that Justice was free. His pass curled deliciously in the air and landed at Justice's feet. But Spencer's job wasn't done yet. He darted down the left side of the field, close enough to the touchline to get chalk on his boots.

Justice's second touch sent the ball back to Spencer, who was by the left goalpost. Spencer reveled in his role as a metronome, dictating the pace of the game. He directed the ball across the face of the goal. Justice took one touch to control it, then shot it past Macintosh into the back of the net.

Spencer cheered along with his team. Micah fist-bumped him, and Justice pulled him into a sweaty hug, but their celebration was cut short.

Coach Schilling blew his whistle. "Goal disallowed."

"What was wrong with it?" Justice planted himself in front of Coach Schilling, hands on his hips.

"The goal was fine, it was the assist," said Coach.

Spencer bent over, hands on his knees, breathing heavily.

"I said two touches. Twinkle Toes here only took one. Let's have a water break."

At the end of practice, Coach Schilling called them all into the team room. Macintosh carried in a cardboard box and placed it on the table in the middle.

"Time for new players to choose jersey numbers," said Coach. "The first one to choose is our man of the match."

Spencer waited for him to call Micah's name, or even one of the twins. But instead he said, "Stand up, Harris."

Spencer's mouth dropped open. The rest of the team clapped for him, and Spencer ducked his head to hide his smile. Macintosh patted him on the back, clearly no hard feelings for getting the ball past him during the game.

Macintosh handed Spencer a piece of paper. It was the

current team roster. He scanned the list, searching for number 10, his old number. A number 10 was the playmaker, the brain of the team, the conductor, the one who controlled the tempo of the game.

He noticed something strange. "There's no number ten," he said.

A muscle in Macintosh's jaw twitched. "That number's retired."

Spencer read the list again. He took his time, searching for the right number. He wasn't a defender, so that eliminated the lower numbers. His eyes settled on number 8 and he smiled. Number 8: the central midfielder. A player who was good on the ball, who created goal-scoring chances for their team by linking the midfield and the attackers, and most of all, had exceptional passing skills. Spencer thought that fit him, both as a player, and a person.

"Number eight? Good choice." Macintosh handed him a blue number 8 jersey. "We'll get your name printed on the back before the first game."

When all the new players had picked their numbers, Coach approached the whiteboard.

"You didn't make this an easy decision for me, but in the end, I need to put the strongest team out there for sectionals this weekend. Other teams will be watching us for weaknesses. But remember, if you don't start, we've still got lots of games to go this year."

Spencer perched on the edge of his seat.

"In goal, we have Macintosh."

Cory's shoulders slumped and he let out an audible sigh, though he must have known he wasn't going to start this game. He held a tissue to his bloody nose, which he got from using his face to stop a ball. It bounced off and the other team still scored.

Coach continued, "We're playing a four-three-three formation." He drew four circles on the board to represent where each player in defense would stand on the pitch as he rattled off their names. He drew three more circles for the midfield.

"In midfield, I'm going with Justice, Zac, and Wyatt."

Spencer's stomach lurched and he looked down at the stained carpet. He thought he'd played well, but clearly it hadn't been enough. What if he never got any game time at all and he was lying to his parents for nothing?

Coach finished the starting lineup. "The rest of you need to keep your head in the game because you could be used as substitutes at any time. Okay, that's it from me. Go home."

Macintosh pulled everyone into a huddle around the table. He put his hands around Spencer's shoulders. On Spencer's other side, Justice did the same. Quickly, the rest of the team joined the huddle. Spencer inhaled the tangy smell of sweat as warm bodies pressed against him. "Welcome to the team," said Macintosh. "You're all Cowboys now; we're all in this together. Where you lead, I will follow."

"Did you just quote both *High School Musical* and *Gilmore Girls*?" asked one of the twins.

"I have older sisters," replied Macintosh. "Anyway, with the talent this team has, I know we can win the League Cup. Let's make it our best year yet."

Though he was disappointed at not making the starting lineup, Spencer still clapped and cheered along with the rest of the team. Everyone from Ms. Greene to his mom and his dad had been telling him that he was going to have a good year, but hearing Macintosh say it while surrounded by his team was the first time that Spencer believed it might actually be true.

Spencer was the last to leave the locker room after practice. He was stuffing his clothes in his backpack when Coach came in.

"Sorry, I thought everyone had left."

"It's just me," said Spencer.

Coach Schilling nodded slightly. "I know you're disappointed, son."

"You didn't have a choice. I messed up in the scrimmage."

"That isn't it. You're a great technical player. You can create chances out of nothing. I wasn't lying when I said we needed you on the team. But the Foxes are an aggressive team and I think right now you lack the physicality to handle them. I'm not about to let you get injured. Not on my watch. That's why I'm not starting you. Hit the gym, wait until your growth spurt, and then I don't think anything will stop you."

He knew Coach was trying to be encouraging, but it wasn't his fault his teammates had at least a two-year head start on puberty.

The funny thing was that on his old team, Spencer was always getting into trouble for being *too* physical. There was one time before he came out and was on the girls' team when he had tackled a girl. She ran toward him and he swung out his foot, making direct contact with the ball.

The referee blew her whistle.

The girl remained on the ground, clutching her leg. There was no way anybody could believe her. She was a better diver than Tom Daley. The referee reached into her pocket and pulled out a yellow card.

"I didn't even touch her," said Spencer.

The referee dipped back into her pocket and pulled out another card. A red one.

His coach marched up to the referee. "You've got to be kidding me. It was a fair tackle!"

The referee wiped her forehead and said, "Ma'am, I'm going to need you both to clear the field."

Spencer began walking off, head bowed in shame. Not because he did anything wrong, but because someone could even think that he would. He was glad his parents hadn't been able to make the game. Dad would probably have told him he needed to pick his battles. Mom would either have wanted to file a complaint about the referee or say that he was overreacting. Spencer wasn't sure which would be worse.

Coach Ireland grabbed his arm, stopping him. "No, you need to review your decision."

"Ma'am, clear the field now or you're getting suspended." Panic hit him like cold water to the face. The team would have no chance if they lost both him and their coach.

"Just because you have a whistle doesn't mean that you're right. No contact was made."

"That's it, you're gone too." The referee motioned for the other officials to escort them off the field. Coach Ireland led Spencer to the bus, where they collapsed into seats.

The silence stretched between them. Spencer swiped the back of his hand over his eyes, wiping away angry tears. It was so unfair. All he'd done was fairly tackle the girl and now Coach Ireland was in trouble as well. If he was in the right, why did he feel so awful? "I'm sorry," he said through the growing thickness in his throat.

Coach Ireland touched his hand. "You have nothing to be sorry for. You did exactly right." To Spencer's surprise and deep mortification, she was crying too. In the three years that she had been his coach, he had never seen her cry. Yell, laugh, cheer, yes. But she always kept a tough exterior that was crumbling right before his eyes.

"I didn't touch her. You taught us not to play dirty like that." A sob escaped his lips.

"I know you didn't. That referee was just trying to show off her power." She put out her arm, laying it next to his. He looked at her skin, brown like his own. She cleared her throat and shook herself. "All right, enough feeling sorry for ourselves. What are you going to learn from this?" she said, starting to sound more like her old self.

"To not make tackles anymore?" suggested Spencer.

She arched an eyebrow and he knew he was wrong.

"And that's going to help us, how?"

He shrugged.

"You keep making tackles, but you have to be smarter. You get the wrong ref and they'll card you for looking at another player the wrong way. Listen, here's the thing: People like you and me are going to have to work a million times harder, be a million times better, and do it without upsetting anybody in order to be successful. It's not fair, but that's just how it is."

They lost the game that day, but Spencer gained a lesson he'd never forget.

"Physicality, my ass," said Aiden, when Spencer explained Coach Schilling's decision over the phone that night. "He hasn't seen you play kickball. I still have a scar from when you tripped me and I fell on a rock."

"That was an accident," exclaimed Spencer. "Anyway, it means that I—" There was a knock on his door and Mom came in.

"Don't mind me."

"Mom, what are you doing?"

"Collecting clothes for a dark wash."

She headed for his laundry basket, which was filled with all his dirty, sweaty clothes from practice.

He leaped off the bed, almost dropping his phone. "Wait!"

She paused, her hand out to the basket.

"I'll do it myself."

"Who are you and what have you done with Spencer?"

"I'm not a baby. I can do my own laundry."

She eyed him suspiciously but left the room, leaving the door partly open behind her. That was a close one. Spencer shut the door and put the phone back to his ear, willing his heart rate to return to normal.

"Sorry."

"What was all that about?" asked Aiden.

"What do you mean?"

"Your voice jumped like three octaves. Wait, your parents still don't know you're on the team, do they? Wow, I'm impressed you managed to keep it secret that long." He chuckled. "And you didn't even need my help. I see my plan of corrupting you is working."

Spencer groaned. "That's actually what I wanted to talk

to you about. I've got a game this weekend. Can I tell my parents we're hanging out?"

"Fine, but if your mom asks, let the record show that I don't approve of your deceit. Hey, I'm busy this week, but let me know when the rest of your games are. I want to come see you play."

Spencer tried to imagine Aiden on the sidelines cheering him on. He was embarrassed to admit that he wasn't sure he wanted him there. Aiden had met Spencer at probably the worst time in his life. And while he loved Aiden for helping him get through it, it wasn't a part of his life he wanted to be reminded of at Oakley.

"You don't want to come. I doubt I'll ever get off the bench." He hoped his voice sounded light and that Aiden couldn't hear his reluctance. "Hey, I still have homework to do. I'll talk to you later."

"Yeah, you should go try to act normal around your mom. No offense, but that was as smooth as chunky peanut butter."

Spencer snickered at that. "Obviously this means you need to do a better job at corrupting me."

After Spencer hung up, he took Aiden's advice and went to the kitchen to check on Mom. He found her making dinner. "Can I help with anything?"

"Sure, you can do the salad," said Mom.

Spencer leaned over her to grab a bowl and she kissed him.

He pulled away, wiping his cheek. "What was that for."

"I appreciate you offering to do your own laundry. It will be a big help for me."

If she knew the real reason, she wouldn't be thanking him.

"It's no problem."

"Who were you on the phone with?"

"Aiden. Can I see him this weekend?"

Spencer didn't miss Mom's pursed lips. He thought the strained relationship between Aiden and his mom was kind of funny, considering they were pretty much the same person. He couldn't go anywhere with either of them without learning the life story of every single person they met.

"Aren't there any friends from school you want to see?"

"I see them five days a week. Please?"

"Is he picking you up?"

"No, I'll ride my bike into town and meet him there."

"Okay. Now, I know Aiden's a little older than you, but neither of your frontal lobes have fully developed."

Spencer rolled his eyes. "My frontal lobes are fine, Mom."

"Just promise me you're not going to do anything impulsive."

Spencer crossed his fingers behind his back. "Promise."

Eight

On Saturday morning, the team piled onto a bus and drove to the rival campus where sectionals were being held. When they arrived, Coach Schilling wasted no time barking out orders, instructing them to change and meet on the pitch in fifteen minutes. Their game wasn't until later that afternoon, but he wanted time to warm up. Plus, it was a good opportunity to judge the competition.

Spencer waited until most of the team left the locker room to start changing. Once dressed, he sat on the bench and pulled out the travel-size first aid kit that Mom made him take everywhere.

He gingerly peeled back the piece of gauze on his heel. The blister had burst and was throbbing painfully.

The door opened. "You ready? Coach is waiting for you," said Justice.

Spencer jumped and quickly pressed the piece of gauze back on his foot.

Justice sucked in a breath. "Ouch, that looks painful."

"It's okay."

Spencer moved to pull his sock on, but Justice stopped him.

"Stay there." Justice picked up Spencer's first aid kit and knelt in front of him on the bench.

He took two fingers and lightly brushed Spencer's foot. "You have to keep this clean, or it will get infected."

Spencer swallowed hard. "I know."

"This might sting." Justice squirted the burst blister with antiseptic spray. He then opened a new piece of gauze and placed it gently across Spencer's heel and wrapped tape around it, before covering it with a larger Band-Aid.

"There. How's that?" He squeezed the top of Spencer's ankle.

Spencer quickly pulled his foot away from where it had been resting on Justice's knee. "Thanks," he said, wincing slightly as he tugged on his too-tight boot.

Justice stood. "Don't mention it. Coach is waiting to start warm-ups. Let's get going before he sends a search party for us."

Spencer limped slightly as he followed Justice out the door.

"Will you be all right to play like that?"

Spencer nodded. Not that he really had a choice.

"I wouldn't say it was bad," said Cory, when they broke practice half an hour later.

Cory was right; it had been horrible. The first drill,

passing, was something Spencer prided himself on being able to do left-footed or right-footed. He swore he could even do it no-footed if it came down to it. He had been wrong. Each step felt like his heel was on fire. It held him back, making his running slow and his passes wildly inaccurate. A bruise bloomed on Cory's cheek where Spencer had pegged him with the ball.

They headed to the sidelines, where some of the soccer moms waited with water and orange slices, but Spencer walked right by them. He mumbled a quick word to Coach about going to the bathroom and rushed off before the tears welling in his eyes could escape.

He waited until he locked the stall before he let himself cry. Loud sobs racked his body and echoed off the tiles in the bathroom. It wasn't just the pain. It was the frustration. He'd been stupid to think he could do this without his family supporting him. He imagined a different scenario where Mom would've taken him to get fitted for new shoes at the start of the season. Theo would be in the stands filming the game for a highlight reel. Dad would be consulting the rulebook and mumbling angrily when referees made the wrong calls. Soccer was their thing, and now it was just Spencer and the bench where he'd sit all game.

The bathroom door opened, footsteps echoed on the tile, then stopped outside his door. "Hey, Spencer, is that you?" Justice was standing outside his stall. "You fall into the toilet or something?"

The door creaked like Justice was leaning on it. "I threw up before my first game for Oakley because I was so nervous."

Spencer sniffed but didn't answer. He didn't want Justice thinking he'd gone and cried like a baby because of a bad practice.

There was a pause, then: "Spence, will you please open the door?"

Spencer wadded up some toilet paper and blew his nose. Then he flushed the toilet and unlocked the stall. He wished he had a cloaking device. It was obvious he'd been crying. His watery eyes and red nose gave it away. But to his surprise, Justice didn't say anything about his face.

"Come on. I have an idea" Justice left the bathroom. Spencer figured that whatever Justice had planned must be better than hanging out alone in a smelly stall.

Justice led him down a flight of stairs and stopped outside of a closed door. For a wild second, Spencer thought that Justice was taking him to Coach Schilling to rat him out for crying in the bathroom. "Where are we going?" he asked.

"It's okay. I know this guy. He helped me out last year after I, you know . . ." Justice mimed hurling. He knocked on the door and a second later a man opened it.

He had a wrinkly neck, a large pockmarked red nose, and a kind smile.

"Justice, you came to visit!" he said in a wheezing voice.

"I told you I would, didn't I?"

The man turned his watery gaze on Spencer. "And who's this?"

Justice pushed Spencer forward into the tiny office. Spencer couldn't walk more than one foot in a straight line without bumping into sports equipment: deflated balls, crushed cones, rusty hurdles.

"This is Spencer. Spencer, this is Sal. He's the grounds-keeper. He's responsible for the amazing fields."

The man took Spencer's hand and gave it a weak squeeze. "I'm afraid the fields aren't up to my usual standards. Some opossums have been getting under the fence and digging holes. I spent all week filling up holes they dug."

"Actually, while opossums do burrow, they aren't known for digging holes," said Spencer.

Both Sal and Justice turned to stare at him. "Sorry, my brother's a big wildlife fan."

"Right," said Sal. "Anyway, staying out of trouble this time, are you? No more messes for me to clean up?"

Justice winked at Spencer. "Now that you mention it, we were hoping we could rifle through lost and found. My man Spence here needs a new pair of cleats."

Spencer didn't know what to think about the "my man" comment.

"Cleats, eh? Check the pile over there. See if you can find your size."

"What size are you?" asked Justice.

Spencer didn't really want to say it out loud. His feet were small for a typical guy his age. "Like six and a half or seven." But Justice didn't say anything as he dug through the pile. He pulled out a pair: black with a green Nike symbol. "Try these."

Spencer tried not to think about the previous owner as he pulled them on. They hugged his feet like old friends.

"How do they look?"

"You look good," said Justice. "I mean, the shoes, they look good. Don't they, Sal?" Justice took a breath, then said, "Will those work, do you think?"

"Yup."

"Great, let's get going, then. It's almost game time."

They thanked Sal and Justice promised to pray for him, then they left, heading up the stairs and back out onto the pitch. Spencer was thankful for the fresh air after being in Sal's stuffy office. Before they reached the field, Justice put his hand on Spencer's arm.

"Listen, next time you have a problem, don't go off crying in the bathroom, okay?"

Spencer lowered his head. He already knew what Justice would say next: Real boys don't cry.

But instead, Justice put a finger under Spencer's chin and lifted his head, so he had no choice but to look into Justice's eyes. A tingling sensation spread from where Justice's skin touched his own.

"I'm your vice captain. If you have something to cry about, you come crying to me. Understand?"

Spencer tried to speak, but his mouth was drier than a dirt field in a drought, so he nodded.

Justice wrapped an arm around his shoulders and they walked back to the pitch together just in time for the game to start.

Nine

Nervous energy surged through Spencer's body like an electric current. He was more anxious watching the game than he ever was playing. At least when he was on the pitch, he could transfer the energy into action, but on the bench, it remained bottled up with nowhere to go. He might as well have been in the stands with the scant crowd of Oakley fans. He crossed his arms and slouched down.

At the pregame pep talk in the locker room, Coach Schilling had said, "I would wish you good luck, but luck is for the unprepared." The four defenders who made up the backline of Oakley's 4-3-3 formation were certainly prepared. They pressed high up the pitch, keeping possession of the ball in the other team's half.

Just before halftime, Micah cut through the Fox defense but missed a gilt-edged chance, sending the ball over the goal. Spencer covered his face with his hands.

At halftime, Coach Schilling stormed into the locker room. His hoodigan hung crookedly on his shoulders. "All of you are making too many mistakes. Micah, what the heck was that? We can't give away chances so cheaply. The next forty-five minutes will determine if we get through to the next round or not. And I don't know about you, but I sure as heck don't want to be eliminated."

Macintosh led the team out to the pitch before the second half. Coach Schilling threw a bib at Spencer. "Start warming up."

Spencer stared at the bib in his hands, then back at Coach Schilling. "You're putting me in?" The fuzzy sound of blood rushing to his head blocked out the noise from the crowd.

"I need you to get in there and create chances for us." Coach Schilling frowned. "You feeling okay? You're looking a little green around the gills."

Spencer shook his head to get rid of the buzzing. This was his chance to prove himself. A mixture of adrenaline and nerves ran through him, but he stretched thoroughly, and then jogged up and down the length of the pitch until he was warm. He shot a glance into the stands, then remembered with a pang that he wouldn't see his parents or Theo with the bright blue ear protectors he always wore to games. One of his favorite parts of games was watching the footage of himself and analyzing it with his mom. But this was another thing he would have to do without her.

Just before the second half started, Coach Schilling signaled to the referee that he wanted to substitute Micah with

Spencer. He pulled Spencer in close. "Go to attacking mid-field and stretch the defense. You need to be an absolute nuisance. Got it?" He clapped a hand on Spencer's back.

The referee blew his whistle to restart the game. The field stretched out around Spencer, seeming ten times more enormous now that he was on it. He was trying to get his bearings when a backward pass from Justice whizzed by him and into the feet of a Fox player, a lithe kid with a number 9 on his back. Number 9 took a shot at goal, but it deflected off the post and rolled out for a goal kick. Spencer's heart nearly jumped out his mouth. He had been on the pitch less than thirty seconds and the other team just got their best chance at scoring.

"Hey, shake it off," called Justice from up the pitch.

Spencer nodded and swiped the back of his hand over his forehead. It was humid for mid-September, and the little wind there was hit him like a puff of warm air. Coach had wanted him to create chances, so that's what he had to do.

The first game he'd ever played was when he was four years old on a co-ed five-a-side rec team. Even then, he shot the ball like an arrow, sending it to where he wanted it to go. But what really set him apart from the other kids was the way everyone else chased after the ball. They wanted to be where the excitement was. But Spencer quickly realized that the place he could do the most good was where the other kids didn't go. On the pitch, he wasn't afraid to be different, and that made him dangerous.

However, when he was four, all the other kids were three

and a half feet tall like him, and not six feet like the Fox player who slid into him, the studs of his boots slamming into Spencer's calf. Pain radiated up his leg and he fell to the ground.

If he was hurt, this was it. He couldn't tell Mom he got injured playing soccer and if she thought that it had happened while he was hanging out with Aiden, then he'd probably never be allowed to see him again.

The ref blew his whistle. Spencer gritted his teeth and rubbed his fingers over the impressions the studs had made in his skin, but no blood appeared. It wasn't as bad as he'd thought. Justice jogged over and put out a hand to help Spencer to his feet.

"Are you okay?"

Justice's touch sent tingles up his arm. Spencer pulled his hand away. There was a place and time, and right now he had a game to win.

The ref showed a yellow card for the late challenge. "Free kick to the Cowboys."

Justice stepped up to the spot marked by the referee. He motioned for Spencer to come to him.

"Remember the video? Watch me. If I raise my right arm, you jump. Got it?" said Justice.

Spencer nodded and went to take his place next to the line of Fox players in the wall. This was his chance. He was the secret weapon.

Spencer was jostled and pushed by sweaty bodies, but he

stood firm and kept his position, all the while keeping his eyes on Justice.

The referee blew his whistle. Justice squinted toward goal and then raised his right arm. Spencer waited until Justice kicked the ball, then he jumped. The Fox players around him jumped as well, and the ball rolled under their feet. Spencer twisted around to catch the goalie diving for it, but he went the wrong way. The ball landed in the back of the net—a winning goal.

The atmosphere in the locker room after the game was electric, with Cory swinging his shirt around over his head while the twins, Zac and Wyatt, performed a tap-dancing routine on the benches. They were one step closer to the finals.

That night, Spencer sat on his bed cradling the lost-and-found boots in his hands. *His* boots now. He rubbed a finger over the stitching. He couldn't get Justice's face out of his head. His smile with the slightly overlapping front teeth, his hair, usually neatly combed except after practice when wind had tossed and tousled it.

There was a knock on the door. Spencer threw the boots under his bed and sat back against the headboard, grabbing his phone and pretending to scroll.

"Come in."

Dad opened the door. Too late, Spencer noticed laces

sticking out from under the bed as Dad came and sat on the edge.

Spencer swung his feet off the bed and casually nudged the laces back under.

"Hey, bud."

"Hey, Dad." Spencer's voice cracked. He cleared his throat.

Dad chuckled. "Mine did that until I was about thirty, so good luck."

"Ha-ha."

"Did you have fun with Aiden?"

"Yeah, it was great."

"Good. Listen, I know this year got off to a bit of a rocky start, what with the soccer team and all that."

Luna strutted through the open door and made a beeline for the aglet of the lace still poking out from under the bed. She began batting it with her paw. Spencer leaned down and pushed the lace completely under the bed, then picked her up. She let out a tortured meow.

Dad continued, "I just want you to know that Mom and I are so proud of how mature and understanding you've been."

The back of Spencer's neck prickled with shame. "Thanks, Dad."

"We know you love soccer, and we're thinking that maybe we could find a co-ed recreational league you could join. Ease into all this. How does that sound?"

"Sounds great," he managed to squeak out.

Dad pulled him into a big bear hug. "I love you, bud."

Spencer swallowed saliva as he hugged him back and said, "Love you too."

Monday morning Spencer walked downstairs to see Theo standing by the front door with his backpack on, even though it wasn't yet time to go to school.

"You're ready early."

"I'm going to do it today," said Theo, not turning to look at him.

"Do what?"

"Ride the bus."

"Good for you," said Spencer as he headed into the kitchen. Since Theo was still refusing to take the bus, Spencer had been riding his bike to school some mornings to help Mom out. But as they were entering the first week of autumn, Spencer frequently arrived at school with his hands frozen to the handlebars and wind-bitten cheeks, wishing for the heated interior of the Subaru.

"I hear today's the day," he said, rummaging in the cupboard for a Pop-Tart.

Mom glanced up at him from where she was flipping through flashcards. "About that, do you think you could take your bike again today?"

Spencer looked down at the unwrapped strawberry

Pop-Tart in his hand. He had hoped to be able to eat it on the way to school, but it seemed like that wasn't happening.

"It will give me time to go through what to expect on the bus again with Theo. Plus, I think if we get him in the car, he won't want to get out."

Spencer stuffed the Pop-Tart back in the box and shoved it into the cupboard.

"Yeah, no problem," he said, still looking away so Mom couldn't see the disappointment on his face. Still, he figured it was the least he could do.

Mom stood and kissed him on the cheek. "Thanks, sweetie. I love you. It's going to be a cold one."

Spencer wiped his cheek. "I'll wear gloves."

As he'd predicted, Spencer arrived at school with his hands frozen to the handlebars. They'd thawed out by lunchtime when he went to the QSA.

"All right," said Grayson, "I've gone over our ideas from our last meeting and I think we should go for creating a proposal for gender-neutral bathrooms."

"Is this up for a vote?" asked a girl who hadn't been at the previous meeting. "It seems silly to spend so much time on something that will only help a few students. If people want a private bathroom they can go in the nurse's office."

"That's miles away from any classroom," said Riley. They raised themselves up taller. "Besides, trans kids have enough to worry about. We shouldn't have to worry about where we pee."

Spencer had been happy to support the initiative in theory, but in practice the idea of bringing awareness to the fact that there were trans students at Oakley made him feel like a spotlight was being shined on him.

"That's true," said Grayson. "Also, think how good it will look on college applications if you can say that you successfully fought for gender-neutral bathrooms in a conservative town."

Spencer had been nodding in agreement at what Riley said, but stopped. Yes, that would be impressive, but his right to pee safely should trump cis people trying to impress colleges. He considered bringing that up, but hesitated. He didn't know these kids that well. He didn't want to rock the boat.

"What about pushback from parents?" asked the girl.

Grayson shrugged. "If it happens, we'll deal with it like we did last year. I'm not too worried."

Spencer sat through the rest of the meeting with a bad taste in his mouth. He was angry at the girl, and Grayson, but most of all, he was angry at himself for not speaking up to back Riley earlier. What kind of friend was he? Moreover, what kind of person was he if he didn't stick up for his own community?

When the meeting ended he wanted to get out as soon as possible, but Grayson stepped in front of him before he could leave.

"So, I've noticed that you're spending more time with Justice Cortes."

"Yeah, we're both on the soccer team." He wondered why it was Grayson's business who he was spending time with.

"Listen, I just want to warn you. His family isn't all that accepting of queer stuff. It was his dad who fought against the dance petition last year. Gender-neutral bathrooms might give his dad a coronary. Just . . . be careful around him, okay?"

"Right, thanks for letting me know." Sure, Justice had been a jerk when they first met, but since then he'd actually been pretty nice.

He was still thinking about Grayson's warning later that afternoon when he sat next to Justice in Music Appreciation. He gave Justice a sideways glance. The thing was, being perfectly nice didn't mean he wasn't homophobic or transphobic.

"Today we begin one of my favorite units." A radiant smile spread across Ms. Hart's face. "We're going to talk about spirituals."

Spencer leaned forward in his seat. Ms. Hart's excitement was infectious. In just a few classes, Music Appreciation had taught him more about other cultures than all his years of social studies combined.

Ms. Hart continued, "Spirituals are songs of faith and resistance, but some historians believe that they were also used by enslaved people to pass secret messages. You've all heard 'Follow the Drinking Gourd,' right?"

There were a few nods.

"I'm going to begin by playing you another song that may have a secret message. This is called 'Steal Away to Jesus.'"

The choir of voices started as a whisper, then swelled into a huge crescendo echoing around the room. Goose bumps peppered Spencer's arms.

The music finished and a hush fell about the room as if nobody dared break the silence.

"What does everyone think?" asked Ms. Hart.

Cole, the boy who had gotten in trouble the first class, raised his hand. "It was okay, but it was sort of repetitive."

"Okay" was the understatement of the year. It was such a simple melody, but the voices electrified Spencer's very core.

"That's a good observation," said Ms. Hart. "Why do you think it's so repetitive? And the words *steal away*, what does that mean?"

Justice raised his hand. "It's obvious. It's about following the words of Christ. And the repetition, well, it emphasizes the importance of living Christ-like."

An uncomfortable feeling twisted inside Spencer. Knowing that Justice was uber-religious and hearing it come out of his mouth were two different things.

Ms. Hart nodded. "That's definitely the literal meaning, but I want you to go deeper. What are some of the hidden messages in the song?"

Spencer was glad that she didn't pick on him. Unlike his white teachers, she didn't expect him to be the Black voice in the classroom, as if he could speak for an entire race.

"Okay, if you're all too shy, I'll tell you. Some say that the words *steal away* referred to going to a secret meeting in the night to plan escapes. Another story says that enslaved people used to sing it to signal that an escape was happening that night. While they worked the fields, one person would start singing and someone else would pick it up, until the message 'steal away' reached every person in that field. Can you imagine how awesome that would be? It demonstrates how a group of voices is stronger than one.

"Today, we're going to look at other code songs. You're going to split into pairs, and I want you to analyze them, looking for possible meanings beyond the literal. Does anybody have questions?"

Justice tapped Spencer's forearm, causing a new crop of goose bumps to erupt. "Do you want to be partners?"

"Sure."

It was an interesting assignment, listening to music, examining the lyrics, and working out hidden meanings. Spencer took the opportunity to study Justice: his long nose, the birthmark on his jawline, the serious look he got on his face when he was paying attention, how he waved his pencil in the air to punctuate what he was saying. How he paused and invited Spencer to talk, asking him his opinions, listening when he disagreed.

The realization hit him suddenly and out of nowhere: He really liked this kid. And a second one, just as sudden: If Justice truly knew who he was, there was a strong possibility that, being from a religious family, he wouldn't like Spencer back.

They finished with twenty minutes left until the end of class. Spencer turned the sheet over and began doodling on the back of it to help clear his mind.

"Hey, where were you at lunch?" asked Justice.

Spencer remembered what Aiden had said about testing people to see if they had a problem with him being queer.

"QSA meeting." It was perfect. There was no way for Justice to know if he was there as a queer or an ally.

"Oh."

Spencer watched for a flicker of anything but saw nothing. He allowed himself to feel some relief.

"You missed Macintosh's speech about regionals and homecoming."

"What about homecoming?"

"We're meeting at his house before the dance for pictures with our dates and then we'll all go together in a limo."

"Hold up, dates?"

"Yeah, dates. For the dance."

"Do you have one?" Spencer thought of Martha from church.

Justice chuckled quietly. "No. My parents don't believe in casual dating. Last year when everyone was taking pictures with their date I took one with my soccer ball. It's kind of become a team joke now."

Spencer laughed too loudly, causing Ms. Hart to glare at them. He ducked his head and pretended to still be working on the assignment. "That's the saddest thing I've ever heard."

"What about you? Do you have a date?"

Spencer quickly sobered up as he thought about getting a date. He wasn't exactly out to the team as queer. Should he ask a guy? Or maybe he and Justice could just hold on to soccer balls together.

He shook his head. "When do we need a date by?" he asked.

"Next Tuesday is the last day to buy tickets,"

"Got it." Spencer added it to his list of worries.

"You look concerned. Do you want to see something that will cheer you up?" Justice passed Spencer his phone surreptitiously. On it was a video of a golden retriever using his snout to score a goal.

"You missed that at lunch too. Then we started talking about which animal we'd choose for what position in a soccer team."

"I know my goalie," said Spencer.

"What?"

"An Andean condor."

"That's oddly specific," said Justice.

"My little brother knows everything about animals. They're one of the largest birds of prey. They've got a huge wingspan and they can fly and dive. Nothing would get by them. What about you?"

"I picked a giraffe. They have long legs."

Spencer barked out a laugh, much louder than before. A few people turned and stared at him. He clapped a hand over his mouth.

"Something amusing, Spencer?" asked Ms. Hart.

"No, sorry."

Justice nudged him. His own face was red from holding in laughter. "What's so funny?"

Spencer couldn't talk for fear of laughing. All he could think about was Cory in goal, looking so much like a bumbling baby giraffe.

Justice nudged Spencer's knee with his own. "Come on, tell me why you're laughing."

"What kind of animal does Cory remind you of?" he asked.

Justice frowned for a second, then his eyes lit up and he let out a chuckle, just as loud as Spencer's. "That's not nice, Spencer," he said.

Spencer jumped when Ms. Hart grabbed the finished assignment from his hands. He tracked her eyes reading the words. She gave the paper back.

"At least you finished your work. However, I'm going to ask both of you to stay after school to tune the guitars. You can continue whatever riveting conversation you're having then."

Despite what Ms. Hart said about continuing their conversation, they worked mostly in silence after Justice taught Spencer how to tune. While he had to use a clip-on tuner, Justice tuned the guitars by ear.

"Do you play?" asked Spencer.

"Yeah, in the praise band at church."

The mention of church brought back Grayson's warning. It seemed like everything in Justice's life revolved around either church or soccer. But how well did he really know him? He needed to find out more about him, and quick, before his crush, or whatever it was, ran away from him. Which meant spending more time with Justice outside of soccer and school.

"What are your plans on Friday?" he asked.

"None, why?"

Spencer gathered up all his courage and blurted, "Do you want to hang out? We could kick a ball around, or see a movie, or get ice cream . . ." Spencer trailed off, feeling his face grow hot. "It's stupid. Never mind."

"Maybe give me a chance to respond?" asked Justice.

"Sorry."

"Is Pelé the best number ten in history?"

"What?"

Justice's eyes twinkled mischievously. "Yes, I'd like to get ice cream."

Ten

The rest of the week, Spencer kept reminding himself that it wasn't a date. They were just two friends going to get ice cream. That's it. Nothing more. But he couldn't ignore the jerk below his navel every time he thought about Justice.

They went to Hartzler's, an ice cream spot in the next town over. Spencer sometimes went there with his family. Mom liked it because it had a playground with a swing that Theo could play on. Dad liked it for the ice cream names. There was the usual chocolate and vanilla, but there was also Chicken Feed (almonds, butterscotch, and brownie in vanilla ice cream) and Moonure (chocolate ice cream with caramel, cheesecake, salted pecans, and dark chocolate chips).

Because it was still warm, they sat at one of the picnic tables next to the playground. "Can I ask you something?" asked Spencer, putting his "is Justice actually a homophobe" plan in motion.

"Shoot," said Justice, taking a bite of his ice cream (Farm House: maraschino cherries in vanilla).

"Don't take this the wrong way, but did your dad really try to stop the QSA from doing the all-gender couples' tickets last year?"

Justice put down his cup. "My family has traditional values that don't always match up with Oakley's progressive views."

"Full offense, that sounds pretty homophobic," said Spencer, not caring if he was being rude.

Justice looked down, not meeting Spencer's eyes.

"I mean . . ." He tried a different tact. "If your parents care so much, why do you even go to Oakley?"

"My mom homeschools the rest of my siblings, but Coach Schilling helped me get a scholarship to Oakley after he saw me play at soccer camp. There's five of us, so an athletic scholarship is pretty much the only way I'll get to college."

"Five?" said Spencer through a mouthful of ice cream (Raspberry Royal: vanilla with raspberry swirls, dotted with chocolate and cashews).

"Two older, two younger. I'm in the middle. What about you? What's your family like?"

"I only have one brother, Theo. He's eight. And my dad's a sociology professor and my mom was an ER nurse."

Spencer caught Justice smiling.

"What is it?"

Justice shook his head. "Your family sounds so normal."

Spencer threw back his head and laughed, thinking of his interracial family with one transgender kid and the other autistic. "You can meet them if you want, and judge for yourself."

"What? Now?" asked Justice.

"Why not? You can come to my house and have a sleepover." Great, now he sounded like a fifth-grade girl inviting someone over for a slumber party.

Justice didn't respond for a couple seconds. Long enough for Spencer to think that maybe he misread Justice's cues, and that he didn't really want to hang out with him.

But Justice grinned at him, his entire face alight. "Yeah, I'd like that. Let me call my parents."

While Justice called, Spencer went inside to use the bathroom. He never got over the nervousness of going into a men's room. He had a strategy, though: He listened outside the door for the sounds within, a stream of pee, a flush of a urinal, or the rush of a faucet. Then, once he felt it was empty, he'd go in, heading for the stall farthest from the door and hoping it wasn't too disgusting. This time, he was in luck. No pee on the seat, no shit in the toilet. He sat down and peed as fast as he could. When he got out, he washed his hands looking down at the sink, not making eye contact as someone else came into the bathroom. He felt his heart rate return to normal as he came back out to the picnic table.

Spencer's house was only fifteen minutes away from the ice cream place. They walked it, since Spencer knew his mom would kill him if she saw him riding in on the back of Justice's bike.

They reached the front door, but before Spencer opened it, he turned to Justice and said, "Remember, my parents don't know I'm on the team, so don't say anything to them about the game this weekend."

"Only talk about soccer with your parents, got it," said Justice, waggling his eyebrows.

"I'm serious," said Spencer.

"Okay, okay, don't talk about anything else besides soccer. I understand, Spencer, I'm not—" His words were muffled by Spencer's hand across his mouth.

Justice curled his hand around Spencer's, lifted it off his mouth, and held it to his chest. "Spencer, I get it. You can trust me."

Spencer wasn't sure he could trust himself. He pulled his hand away from Justice's chest and opened the front door.

"Spencer, sweetie, is that you?" called Mom.

He caught Justice's smirk. He'd have to have a talk with her about calling him "sweetie."

"Yeah, it's me."

Mom came into the hall.

"Mom, remember Justice? Can he stay for dinner and sleep over?"

She opened and closed her mouth a few times. It had been a while since Spencer had invited a friend over, but did she have to be so obvious?

"Mom?"

Mom cleared her throat. "Of course he can."

Spencer took Justice's arm and pulled him into the living room, away from Mom, but she followed behind them. "Can I get you anything? Pop, chips?"

Justice opened his mouth to speak, but Spencer cut him off. "We're fine." He hoped she'd take the hint and leave them alone.

"I'm just so pleased to see Spencer is making friends," said Mom, her voice breaking like she was about to cry.

"Mom, actually could we have some pop?" He wanted her out of the room before she started blabbing to Justice about how he was an antisocial hermit.

"Of course."

Justice sat on the couch besides Theo, who was watching TV. "*Planet Earth*?" said Justice. "I love that show."

"The weird boy sits on the couch and tries to talk," said Theo, in a scarily accurate David Attenborough impersonation.

Justice turned to Spencer.

"Yeah, he does that sometimes." Spencer went into the kitchen to see where Mom was with the pop. She was leaning against the cabinet wiping her eyes. "Are you crying?"

Mom fanned her face. "I'm sorry. I'm just happy that you're happy."

Spencer scuffed the floor with his toe. "It's not a big deal."

Mom blew her nose on a paper towel. "Okay, now let's set ground rules."

"Mom, not now." He sort of wished she would go back to crying.

"He's sleeping on the air mattress," said Mom.

"Duh," said Spencer.

"In the living room," she added.

"Fine."

The front door opened and Dad's voice boomed into the kitchen. "Whose death machine is parked in my driveway?"

Spencer and Mom met him in the hall.

"Spencer has a friend over."

"Friends? What friends?" said Dad.

Justice peeked his head out of the living room. "Sorry, I'll move my bike if it's in the way." He started toward the door, then stopped outside of Dad's home office. "Is that your guitar, Professor Harris?"

Spencer was impressed that Justice remembered what his dad did. Dad seemed momentarily stunned, but he quickly recovered. "Betty, yeah, she's mine."

Betty was his dad's prized Martin guitar.

"You play?"

"A little," said Justice.

"Go on and take her down. Show me what you got."

Spencer watched in amazement as Justice lifted Betty off of her stand and put the strap over his shoulder. Spencer got yelled at for looking at her the wrong way.

Justice strummed a few chords, then jumped into an intricate finger-picking tune.

Dad leaned against the wall and nodded along. "I always wished one of my kids would be musical, but they both inherited Connie's ear. Don't tell her I said that."

"Hey," said Spencer. Though he had endured years of off-key lullabies.

Justice laughed. "I don't know. I've heard him sing. He's not too bad."

Dad raised his eyebrows. "Sing? My son?" He and Justice laughed.

Spencer rolled his eyes. "I'll just leave you two alone, then, since you both seem like you're having so much fun."

"Spence, wait." Justice took off the guitar and carefully handed it back to Spencer's dad. "Thanks, Professor Harris." He caught Spencer's arm before Spencer got too far down the hall. "No offense to your dad, but I'd much rather spend time with you."

They headed back to the living room. Spencer sat next to Theo on the couch and Justice sat on Theo's other side.

"So, Theo," said Justice. "Spencer says you like animals. What's your favorite?"

"Oh, dear," said Spencer, putting his hand in front of his mouth to hide his smile

"What did I say?" asked Justice, eyebrows raised.

"I don't have a favorite because every animal has evolved differently to adapt to their environment," said Theo.

"Ah, I see," said Justice. "Do you have a least favorite, then?"

Theo turned off the TV. "I'm going to go watch in my room." He left.

Spencer laughed.

"Did I do something wrong?"

"Theo doesn't have much patience for stupid questions. Don't worry, you get used to it."

"I didn't think I was asking a stupid question," said Justice.

Spencer started to respond but stopped when he recalled Theo's comment. "Wait, don't take this the wrong way, but you do believe in evolution, right?"

Justice blinked in surprise. "Yes, I believe in evolution." He smiled as if he was remembering something funny. "Actually, sometimes I pretended I didn't just to annoy my biology teacher my first year. He had this vein that popped out in his forehead when he'd argue with me. He begged me to switch when I signed up for his earth sciences class. He probably thought I'd argue about how old the Earth is."

Spencer wasn't sure if he should laugh or not. Luckily Mom called them from the kitchen for dinner, where Justice patiently answered his parents' questions and Spencer was spared hearing too many embarrassing childhood stories about himself.

After dinner Dad found the air mattress they used for guests and Spencer got the pump from the basement. Once it was blown up, he grabbed extra sheets from the cupboard on the second-floor landing and made the bed. Mom said

Justice had to sleep in the living room, but she never said anything about him sleeping in his own bed, so he grabbed a pillow and blanket for himself and draped it over the couch.

Justice came out of the bathroom wearing a pair of Dad's pajama pants. He had tried on a pair of Spencer's first, but they had been ridiculously short on him. Justice spread out on the mattress and rolled over to face Spencer.

"Are you tired?" asked Justice.

Spencer tore his eyes away from the soft, pale skin above Justice's hipbones where his T-shirt had ridden up. He hoped Justice hadn't noticed. "Not yet, you?"

"Nope."

They fell into silence. The only sound was the chirping of crickets outside. Spencer's stomach gurgled and he covered it with a cough.

Justice tried to hide his smile.

Spencer searched for something to say that would break the awkwardness. "Are you still hungry?"

Justice shrugged.

"If I made popcorn, would you eat it?"

"Is Pep Guardiola the greatest coach in the modern game?"

"I'll take that as a yes."

Spencer jumped off the couch. He leaned down and put out his hand to Justice, who grasped it. Friends helped friends get up all the time. It wasn't a big deal.

In the kitchen, Justice leaned against the counter while

Spencer searched for the popcorn. He spotted it high on a top shelf. He judged the distance and how stupid he'd look if he had to find a step stool to reach it. He turned to Justice. "Could you grab me the popcorn from up there?"

"Sure." Justice reached up and got it, but he didn't give it to Spencer. Instead he held it up above Spencer's head.

Spencer hopped up to reach it. "Come on, give it to me!"

Justice laughed at him and raised it higher.

"Fine, no popcorn."

"Yes, how will I, a Luddite who doesn't believe in evolution, ever put this in the microwave without your help, oh enlightened one."

"Hey, my question about evolution was a fair one given what you told me about your family's 'traditional values.'"

Justice dropped the box in Spencer's hands. Spencer set the microwave going and leaned against the counter next to Justice.

"But seriously, you believe in evolution, but what about other people in your church? Like Martha?"

"Well, maybe not Martha. But it's tough being the pastor's kid."

Spencer asked the question he'd been wanting answered for a while. "Are you two, like, have you—"

Justice let out a bark of laughter. "Me and Martha? No. Though, I'm sure our parents wouldn't mind if we did. But I'm not interested in dating anybody. I need to concentrate on soccer."

Even though Spencer already knew he didn't have a chance with Justice, that confirmation felt like a punch to the gut. The microwave dinged, so he took out the popcorn and gave it to Justice to pour into a bowl.

They moved back into the living room and sank onto the couch with the bowl of popcorn between them.

"We could stream a movie," suggested Spencer. "Choose whatever you want." He handed Justice the remote.

Justice flipped through the screens for several minutes, his brow furrowed.

"I'd like to watch one preferably before next year," said Spencer.

"This is a lot of pressure," said Justice.

"What is?"

"I don't know any of these and I want to pick a movie you'll like." Spencer melted, until Justice continued with, "You strike me as a musical comedy with a happy ending type of guy."

"Seriously?"

"Yeah, you're sensitive, like you care about people. But you're also kind of goofy."

"Well, you strike me as a tear-jerking made-for-TV inspirational sob story type of guy," said Spencer with a grin.

"You got me," said Justice, smiling back. "But seriously, what do you want to watch?"

"I don't mind."

"What about a scary movie? Or will you have nightmares?"

"No," Spencer lied. "Besides, if I do, I've got you to protect me."

The tips of Justice's ears turned red. "I'm a midfielder. Not exactly defense material. How about this one?"

Spencer read the description out loud. "'*The Mannequin Massacre*: Shoppers vanish from the streets of New York City, and their bodies show up in high-end storefronts as mannequins.'" He quirked an eyebrow at Justice. "This sounds ridiculous."

Justice patted Spencer's knee and Spencer jumped. "Scared already?"

"Shut up."

The movie was laughably bad. There were a few jump scares that caught both him and Justice by surprise, and they grinned sheepishly at each other in the dark. At one point, Spencer's hand brushed Justice's in the popcorn bowl. He pulled it away quickly and glanced at Justice, but he continued to stare straight at the TV.

When it was over, and the popcorn was finished, Justice moved to the air mattress and Spencer stretched out on the couch.

Spencer lay on his back, looking at the shadows on the ceiling. He was still bursting with energy.

The air mattress squeaked as Justice rolled over and

propped himself up on his elbow. Spencer could make out the outline of his features in the dark.

"So, do you still think my family is normal?" asked Spencer.

"Your dad is something else. You're a lot like him."

Spencer shifted. This pleased him. He'd always been compared to his mom. "You think?"

"Yeah, both got big ears."

"You know what they say about big ears," said Spencer.

"Can you not?" said Justice, throwing a pillow at him.

"Thanks, now I've got two pillows and you've got none." Spencer said, half hoping, half daring Justice to try and get it. When he didn't, Spencer threw it back.

Justice yelped, and Dad called, "Don't make me come down there," sending them both into giggles.

"Are they weirder than yours?" Spencer whispered.

"I'm the weird one in my family," said Justice.

Spencer found that hard to believe. How could the all-American good old boy be the weird one?

Justice rolled over and yawned. "I'm tired. Good night, Twinkle Toes."

For once that name made him smile. "Night, Justice."

Spencer jerked awake to see a figure looming over him. He screamed, thinking the Mannequin Murderer had climbed out of the TV. Then someone clapped a hand over his mouth.

Justice shushed him. "It's only me." He took his hand away. "I think the mattress has a hole in it."

Sure enough, the mattress had deflated, collapsing in on itself. Spencer attributed the next words that came out of his mouth to the loss of blood to his brain from the adrenaline rush. He scooted over on the couch. "Grab your pillow and come here."

Justice raised an eyebrow at him. "Are you sure?"

"Yeah, there's plenty of room."

"I'm too tired to argue with you." Justice climbed in next to him. Spencer jumped when Justice's cold foot slid against his calf.

"Sorry," said Justice.

"It's all right." Spencer closed his eyes. He pressed a hand to his pounding heart and tried to convince himself it was just from his near-death experience.

Theo's iPad was inches away from Spencer's face the next time he opened his eyes. He moved, and felt Justice stir beside him.

"Oh, you're not dead," said Theo. He sounded sort of disappointed as he sat down on the couch and turned on the TV.

Spencer yawned and rubbed his eyes. Suddenly, he became aware that he was using Justice's shoulder as a pillow, and Justice was awake.

Spencer struggled to sit up. "Sorry, I didn't mean to sleep on you. Why didn't you move?" he asked.

"I didn't want to wake you," said Justice.

"I'm trying to watch TV here," said Theo.

Justice excused himself to go to the bathroom. Spencer wrapped the blanket around himself, missing Justice's warmth.

Theo looked at him. "Do you love Justice?"

Spencer coughed. "No, why?"

"You were sleeping with him."

"Because the mattress broke."

"Did you know that beavers mate for life?"

"I do now."

Spencer remembered Mom's rules about Justice sleeping on the blow-up mattress and her comment about him and Justice engaging in certain behavior. He didn't want to involve Theo, but . . .

"Hey, buddy, don't tell Mom about what you saw, okay?"

"Okay."

"Promise?"

"I promise."

After breakfast, Spencer walked Justice to the door and watched him ride away with a smile on his face. The smile slid off when he found Mom in the kitchen.

"So, the mattress broke, huh?"

Spencer glared at Theo, who was innocently munching

on toast. "I didn't tell her, I showed her." He pointed to his iPad.

And that was how Spencer ended up chasing Theo around the kitchen yelling at him to delete the footage or he'd smash the iPad until Mom got in the middle of them.

"Theo, delete it. Spencer, listen, he seems like a nice boy, but not everyone will understand."

"I know."

"You need to be careful."

"It's not like that. We're friends, that's all." But that night, as he stuffed his face in his pillow, inhaling Justice's soapy, woodsy scent, he knew that he was a goner.

Eleven

At lunchtime on Tuesday Justice leaned over and stole a baby carrot from Spencer's lunch box. Spencer swatted his hand away.

Justice held the carrot between his two teeth and dangled it at Spencer, which was kind of gross, but also kind of adorable, and should totally not cause Spencer to feel that way about his teammate.

Macintosh called down the lunch table. "Tomorrow we're eating in the team room to go over footage for regionals this weekend. Also, has everybody bought homecoming tickets? Today's the last day."

And crap. Spencer had been so caught up about his not ice cream date with Justice that he completely forgot about finding a real date for homecoming.

Spencer spoke. "What if we don't have a date?"

Macintosh pointed his fork at Justice. "I'm sure Cortes can give you some tips." He froze, fork still dangling in the air, then lifted an eyebrow and glanced between Justice and Spencer. "Listen, hear me out. Why don't you two go together?"

The carrot dropped from Justice's mouth onto the table.

Macintosh continued, "Look, no offense, but neither of you are going to get real dates and today's the last day to buy tickets. I'm not saying that you'll go *together* together, but why don't you buy your tickets now as a pair to get the cheaper price?"

"Can guys even buy a couples' ticket?" asked Micah.

"Yeah, Grayson petitioned for it last year," said Macintosh.

Spencer tried to look at Justice, but he avoided his eyes.

"This will be hilarious," said Cory. "Are you going to buy Spencer a croissant?"

"A what?" asked Justice. He crossed his arms tight against his chest.

"You know, that flower bracelet thingy."

"You mean a corsage, dickwad," said Micah.

"How would I know what they're called?"

"Guys, stop," said Spencer. "We're not going together."

Justice was glowering at the table as if it had insulted his mother.

The warning bell rang and there was a shuffle of bags and trays as everybody got up. Justice cleared out before Spencer could talk to him.

. . .

For the rest of the afternoon, Spencer thought about what he would say to Justice when he saw him again in Music Appreciation. He could try to make it a joke, like "Oh, that Macintosh." But when he entered the classroom, he saw that Justice was sitting at the opposite end of the circle than they normally did, and Spencer spent the rest of the class trying to pretend like the snub didn't sting.

When the bell rang, Spencer rushed out to avoid seeing Justice. He was partway down the hall when a hand touched his arm to stop him.

"Hey," said Justice.

"Hi."

"Look." Justice took a deep breath. "Do you want to go to homecoming? Together?"

Spencer focused on the scuffmarks on the floor. He tried to remain calm even though his heart was doing bicycle kicks in his chest. Justice was probably asking to save money on tickets. It didn't mean anything. "I guess. I mean, the tickets are cheaper."

"I can buy the tickets."

"No, it's okay."

"You bought the ice cream."

"Okay, yeah."

"Yeah?"

. . .

That evening, Spencer tried on the suit Mom had bought him only a few months ago for his aunt's wedding. At first he thought he'd gotten it from Theo's closet by mistake because the pants ended at his ankles and the suit jacket hit above his wrists. His growth spurt chose the wrong time to happen.

Dad's office door was closed, which meant he was working on a lecture and didn't want to be disturbed, but Spencer knocked anyway. This was an emergency.

"What?" Dad growled like a bear being roused too early from hibernation. Spencer pushed the door open and went in. Dad sat behind his desk squinting at his computer screen. Books were piled up high next to him.

"I need a new suit for homecoming."

Dad didn't look up. The light from the computer screen reflected in his glasses. "We'll go on the weekend." When Spencer didn't leave he said, "Anything else?"

"Dad, can I ask your advice?"

"As long as it's not about math."

"I'm sort of going to the dance with Justice, but—"

"Oh, Justice. He's a cool kid." Dad's expression changed as Spencer's words sunk in. "Are you two dating or something?"

Spencer's face grew hot. "That's what I need advice on." He was pretty sure they were going as friends. But then there were those little moments, those glances, those touches that made him think it could be something else. "How do you know if someone's interested in you?"

"A guy, you mean?"

"Well, yeah."

Dad took off his glasses and rubbed the bridge of his nose where they had made an indent. "Bud, I need to finish this lecture for tomorrow if I'm going to make enough money to buy you suits. Maybe you should ask your mom about your guy problem?"

"Oh, right." He shut the door to Dad's office, but instead of searching out Mom, he went back upstairs to his room. He'd never questioned his parents' love for him. They voted for liberal candidates, and when he was six and one of Dad's colleagues was getting married, they'd explained to Spencer that men can marry men and women can marry women because love is love.

But sometimes Spencer wondered if they really believed it or were just saying what they thought was the right thing. He wasn't sure if parents had limits to their love, but he was worried that one day something would push them too far and he'd find out.

That Friday Mom asked over dinner, "Got your bag packed for tomorrow?"

Spencer jumped, scaring Luna the tabby, who had been sitting under his seat waiting for him to sneak her some asparagus off his plate. His soccer bag was packed and ready to go for when Aiden picked him up to take him to regionals tomorrow, but Mom couldn't know that.

"What bag?" he asked, deciding to play innocent.

"We're going to Akron for your appointments, remember?"

"That's tomorrow?" His stomach rolled uneasily. Once a month they drove up to Akron Children's Hospital to meet with his medical team for a day full of appointments.

"Yes. Bring your homework so that you can get started on it. And remember, no food after nine tonight."

There was no way getting out of it and he knew it was important, but the game was important as well. He could tell Coach he was sick, but then he'd probably require a note or something. Spencer decided he wasn't going to do anything and face the repercussions on Monday.

So on Saturday morning while the team was on the bus on their way to the game, Spencer sat on the highway with his mom. Instead of warming up, he flicked through a magazine in the doctor's office waiting to do blood tests, his phone screen flashing every few minutes with calls and texts until he turned it off.

As the phlebotomist slipped the needle into the crook of his elbow to draw blood, the referee stood in the middle of the pitch and blew his whistle to start the game.

It would have been halftime by the time he met with his endocrinologist, who asked him questions.

"Any bleeding?"

"No."

"Side effects?"

"Just acne."

"I'll write you a prescription for a retinoid that'll clear it right up."

Then back to the waiting room, still not brave enough to turn on his phone, before seeing his therapist and talking about how school's going, and whether he's making friends, without being able to mention the soccer team, or Justice. He didn't like keeping things from her, but the fewer people who knew about his lies, the better.

Then they were back in the car on the way home. The game was over and he didn't know if they won or lost.

It wasn't until that evening that he finally screwed up the courage to check his phone. His palms grew clammy as dozens of missed calls and texts flashed across the screen. Most were from Justice. Spencer held his phone at arm's length as if the distance would make the texts less painful to read.

Justice: Where are you?

Justice: I'm trying to hold the bus

Justice: We had to leave, sorry. See you at the game?

Justice: Seriously? You're just not going to show?

Justice: We won. No thanks to you.

He deflated onto the bed. He wished that it didn't have

to be like this, that he could spend his Saturday like everyone else and not be poked with needles and asked awkward questions, but also knowing that doing so probably saved his life.

Still, he owed Justice and the whole team an explanation. Before he could figure out what to say Mom called him downstairs.

He checked the time on his phone; it was a bit early for dinner. He scrubbed his face, as if he could wipe away the guilty feeling, and dragged himself downstairs. Mom and Dad were in the dining room, Mom's phone on the table between them.

He slid into a seat on the opposite side of the table, feeling a bit like a suspect in the cop procedurals Mom watched while folding laundry.

"What's up?" he asked lightly. Mom's raised eyebrow told him this had been a mistake.

"Care to explain this?"

Mom played her voicemail. Coach's gruff voice came through the speaker. "Hello, Mrs. Harris. This is Coach Schilling. I'm calling to see where Spencer is. We've got a game this morning. Hope everything is okay."

He wilted under her unflinching stare. He glanced at Dad for support, but even Dad, who usually performed the role of good cop, eyed him with a steely gaze.

"Well . . ." said Mom.

He could lie. He could say he was supposed to film the game for AV club. But what if they talked to Coach? One lie, they might forgive, but get caught again and he would be doomed.

Then he thought about the other people involved: Aiden, Theo, even Justice. Spencer knew he had to take responsibility.

He took a deep breath. "I joined the soccer team."

"You mean you went behind our backs and joined the team after we expressly told you not to," said Mom. He had braced himself for an explosion, but Mom's voice came out quiet and controlled, almost like she was explaining a math equation to him.

Her apparent calmness grated. He'd only lied because they were being unreasonable, not even considering letting him play. And the reason they wouldn't let him play was because it was a boys' team.

As if proving Spencer's point, Dad said, "I don't get it, Spence. We only wanted you to wait. You could've joined a co-ed team next semester."

Spencer raised his arms in frustration. There it was. "I don't want to join a co-ed team. I'm a boy. I want to play on the *boys' team*. Why don't you get that?"

Mom opened her mouth to speak, but Spencer plowed on. Everything he'd wanted to say whenever they misgendered or deadnamed him bubbled to the surface. "I'm sorry

I'm not your little girl anymore, but honestly, I never was and you both need to accept that."

A small part of him enjoyed the look of hurt that flashed across their faces. Good. Now they understood a fraction of the pain that he felt.

His chest heaved and he felt suddenly exhausted: from the day of appointments, the anxiety of facing the team on Monday, and the inevitable punishment he was bound to receive. He pushed back his chair and stormed upstairs, ignoring his parents' calls behind him.

Twelve

Punishment came swiftly. On Sunday Mom and Dad ambushed him in his bedroom early and doled out his sentence. He was grounded for the foreseeable future. No soccer, no Aiden, and certainly no Justice.

On Monday morning Mom came with him to apologize to Coach Schilling and officially quit the team. She did most of the talking while Spencer stared at the ground, only risking the occasional glance at Coach Schilling, then looking away just as quickly when he saw the crushing disappointment etched into his features.

He didn't want to face the team at lunch, so he went to the library instead, nibbling on carrots when the librarian wasn't looking.

But he couldn't avoid Justice in Music Appreciation.

Spencer had waited until the last possible moment but Justice still managed to corner him outside the classroom.

He scowled at Spencer. "You owe me an explanation."

"I had a doctor's appointment," said Spencer weakly.

Justice wasn't moved. "Why didn't you tell someone? You

were going to start. We had to rearrange the whole game plan."

"I forgot about it until Friday." That was true. He'd been so busy it had completely slipped his mind. Besides, if he had told them, then they might have asked questions. Questions that Spencer didn't want them knowing the answers to.

Justice shook his head. "Maybe soccer is just a fun after-school activity for you, but for the rest of us, it means something. This is Macintosh's last chance to win the cup, and for me . . ." He trailed off. "For me it's my way out. If you're not serious about playing, we don't need you." Justice swept into the classroom, leaving Spencer in the hallway.

The only positive of the whole situation was spending more time with Riley, who usually ate lunch backstage with the other theater kids but had offered to sit with Spencer in the cafeteria after seeing him go into the library by himself several lunch periods in a row.

Riley was happy to scribble costume sketches while Spencer stewed, and they didn't mind that Spencer only answered in monosyllables, but even they noticed when Justice shot a dirty glare at their table while throwing away his trash.

It was wild hair day for homecoming week. Not feeling the homecoming spirit, Spencer had ignored the themed days, but Justice's normally neat hair was styled up in a

Mohawk. Spencer had watched one of the soccer girls do it before school. He wondered whether Justice was going to take her to homecoming instead of him now that Spencer was grounded and Justice hated him.

"What did you do to anger soccer Jesus?" asked Riley.

"What?" Spencer tore his eyes away from the soccer table where Justice was now officiating an intense thumb war between Micah and Cory.

Riley blushed. "That's what I call Justice. You used to be all buddy-buddy, but now he's acting like you killed his cat."

Spencer explained what happened with the soccer team and his parents. Riley was an attentive listener, nodding sympathetically at the right moments and raising their eyebrows when Spencer reenacted the blow-up at his parents.

"Wow, you said that to them?"

"I've been out almost three years and sometimes they act like they just found out. I want them to stop holding me back."

"Did you tell *that* to them?" asked Riley pointedly.

"No, why?"

Riley pushed a strand of hair back. "I don't know your parents, but it sounds like they're trying to protect you in their own way."

"I guess."

"But maybe if you explain that by taking you off the team to protect you, they're actually hurting you, they'll understand."

Spencer considered that for a moment while Riley continued.

"Like, take homecoming. My parents wanted me to wear really gendered clothing because they think that if I show up in something too out there, I'll be a target."

Riley caught Spencer staring at their ratty hoodie. "I don't wear this for fashion. It's more like armor. I already know I'll be a target if I show up in what I really want to wear. But at homecoming everybody else will be looking their best, and I'm not going to waste it squeezed into some uncomfortable outfit because of cisnormativity."

"So what do you think I should do?"

"Show your parents what you're missing out on by not being on the team, then maybe they'll understand and let you rejoin."

"I doubt the team will want me back."

Riley flipped to a new page in their sketchbook. "Well, did you apologize for missing the game? You did sort of leave them out to dry."

Riley took Spencer's silence as a no. "There's your answer. Apologize to the team and show them why they need you back."

Doubt crept into Spencer's head. Did the team need him? They'd already won without him. But if they didn't need him, why was Justice so pissed? Why did he feel Coach Schilling watching him during PE? He considered himself pretty average, but soccer was the one place he excelled.

He could maneuver the ball in unimaginably tight spaces. He could decode patterns that other people didn't see.

Excitement drummed in his chest. "I think I have an idea. But I need to get old video from the team room."

"I can help. I'm on AV club. I'll tell Coach Schilling I'm putting together a highlight reel of last season."

Later that day Riley slipped Spencer a USB drive with last year's game from the team they were playing on Friday. It was only a friendly that took place on homecoming before the football game, but it was what Spencer needed.

He spent the night bent over his laptop poring over the footage, continuously rewinding, searching for anything that could help the team win. After several hours, he found what he was looking for. He spliced together the footage and added captions before saving and uploading it. He texted the link to Justice and Macintosh before crawling into bed, eyes aching with tiredness.

For his parents, he took a different approach. He dug up the footage that Theo filmed on a shaky iPad camera from the time when he was big enough to hold one. Footage of Spencer playing soccer when he was younger, or kicking a ball with Dad. He added pictures of himself and his teammates hanging out, going for pizza after winning, comforting each other after losing. Everything that represented what being on the team meant to him. He didn't know if it would work, but it was worth a shot.

. . .

The night of homecoming he lay on his beanbag playing FIFA. Mom had gone to one of her mom support groups. Spencer couldn't keep up with how many she belonged to now. Maybe this one was for parents of liars.

There was a knock on his door and Theo came in.

"Do you want to be in my movie?" he asked.

There were certainly worst ways he could spend homecoming than making a movie with his little brother.

In Theo's movie, Spencer played a squirrel who was trying to hide his acorns before a fox (played by Luna the cat) could get them. Theo had even made a construction paper tail and ears for Spencer and was directing him on how to be more squirrelly when the doorbell rang. Spencer opened the door. Standing outside his house was Justice in a suit.

"Nice ears," said Justice.

Spencer ripped the ears from off his head. "What are you doing here?"

"Picking you up for homecoming." Justice scanned the rest of Spencer's outfit: gray sweatpants and a wrinkled T-shirt. "You might want to change. I don't think that meets the dress code."

Spencer shook his head in confusion. "Yeah, but why are you doing this?"

"Your video analysis worked." Justice smirked. "Offside trap. Risky, but effective. Thank you."

Spencer stared at the ground. "You could've thanked me at school on Monday."

"I know, but I was getting ready with the team and we decided it didn't feel right that you weren't there." He lowered his voice. "Plus, I'd really like to take you to homecoming."

Before Spencer could overanalyze what he meant, Dad came up behind him. "Close the door. I'm not paying to heat the whole neighborhood, Spence. Oh, hello."

"Hi, Professor Harris. I'm here to pick Spencer up for homecoming," said Justice.

"I'm sorry, I can't go," said Spencer, pretty sure that being grounded meant not being able to go to homecoming with cute boys from the soccer team.

Spencer began to shut the door but Dad held an arm out. "Wait." He chewed on his bottom lip. "Give him fifteen minutes."

"Here, you can be in my movie," said Theo, taking Justice's hand and pulling him inside.

"Come on, let's get you dressed," said Dad.

Spencer followed him upstairs. "But I don't have anything to wear."

"Let me see if I have something that might work." He began taking jackets with hangers out of his closet. He handed one to Spencer. "Go try it on." He sniffed the air. "On second thought, jump into the shower for thirty seconds."

"Why are you doing this?"

"I'm being your wingman."

This didn't make sense. Just a few days ago Dad was telling him to talk to his mom about boys, and now he was trying to get Spencer ready for a date? "But I thought I was grounded."

"If you're home by ten, Mom won't know and I promise not to tell her. Now go get cleaned up."

Spencer thought he was done with keeping secrets from his parents, but he figured he could make one last exception. He sped through his shower on autopilot, so distracted that he washed his body with hair conditioner and had to rinse off and start again. He was going to homecoming. With a boy! And not any boy, either. Justice, who apparently didn't hate him. Plus, Dad was being weirdly cool about the whole thing.

Once he'd toweled off, he tried on the clothes Dad laid out for him. He found a jacket that wasn't too long, and a pair of his own dark jeans that would have to do. He went back to his parents' room, where Dad was waiting for him.

"This will work for tonight. We can get it tailored later. Every man should have a tailored jacket." He tackled Spencer's hair with a comb and hair gel. Spencer winced as Dad ran the comb through his curls.

When Spencer's hair was done, Dad draped a blue-and-green paisley tie over Spencer's shoulders. "This was my father's. He didn't have many opportunities to wear it. When he did, he tied it like this." He looped the wide end around the skinny end twice, poking it through the hole in the neck, and tugged it tight. "This is called the four-in-hand. It's a useful knot. If you want something a little classier, try this."

His hands flew so fast, Spencer couldn't see what he was doing until he created a large symmetrical knot.

Spencer laughed. "That knot is almost the size of my head."

"It's called the full Windsor. I think it's something you'll grow into. Now, this is how I tie my tie." He undid it again. This time, he put the tie around Spencer's neck with the underside facing up.

"You're only going to move the wide end. The narrow end gets held in your hand, like this. Go around once, around again, up, over, and through." He tugged, leaving Spencer with a knot that was larger than the four-in-hand and smaller than the full Windsor, but still symmetrical. "How's that?"

Spencer adjusted the knot so that it was straight and looked at himself in the mirror.

"I like it. Will you do it again, slower?"

Dad nodded and undid the knot, then showed him again. "Now you try," he said.

Spencer took both ends and tried to mimic what Dad had done. He got lost a couple times, but Dad's hands guided his own. He ended up with a solid knot.

"Just like that. You're a natural."

"Did your dad teach you how to tie a tie?" asked Spencer.

"He did, just before I went to college. He thought it'd help me fit in better with all the white boys.

"I was the first in my family to go to college. My dad had a bit of an idealized view. In his mind it would be old, ivy-covered buildings, majestic libraries, and grassy quads. In reality it was late nights out and going to class with a hangover.

"The first time I actually needed to wear a tie was for his funeral. I think it would mean a lot to him to know that you're wearing it now."

Spencer had never met his grandfather, but sometimes he examined himself in the mirror and recognized the sticky-out ears and full bottom lip from the photo on the mantelpiece and wondered whether his grandpa would accept him being transgender. In that moment, he knew that Dad was talking about more than ties.

Spencer buttoned his jacket and was about to leave when Dad stopped him. "Whoa, there. You can't go out like that."

Spencer scanned himself. The navy jacket fell across his shoulders almost perfectly and tapered in slightly at the waist. His jeans were skinnier than he was used to, but that only showed off his filled-out soccer thighs. "What's wrong?"

Dad reached down and unbuttoned the bottom button of his jacket. "I know this is silly, but you only ever fasten the top button of a two-button jacket. You button it when you stand and unbutton it when you sit down. But under no circumstances do you fasten the bottom button."

"Why not?"

"There was a fat king who said so."

"What?"

"Spencer, we don't have time. Your Prince Charming is waiting."

Dad dropped them off at Macintosh's. He lived in a swanky neighborhood a few towns over. His house was a new-build McMansion that would stick out among the homes in Spencer's modest neighborhood. Justice got out of the car.

Before Spencer could get out Dad said, "Remember, home by ten. Any later and you're on your own with Mom." Dad squeezed his shoulder. "Follow your heart, okay?"

Outside, some of the soccer team passed a ball around the manicured lawn in their suits. They stopped when they saw Spencer and rushed toward him, hugging him and slapping him on the back. He liked the feeling of being part of the team again.

Macintosh pulled him aside. "No hard feelings, Twinkle Toes. Your offside trap was genius. Of course, Cortes didn't want to do it until we were losing in the second half, but once we did it, it worked a charm." He winked at Spencer. "Okay, now that Mr. and Mr. Cortes-Harris are here, we can do pictures."

Spencer's cheeks burned. He sometimes got the idea

that Macintosh knew how he felt about Justice. After all, he made them be partners in the three-legged race in the first practice. And it was his idea for them to go to homecoming together. But the best way to deal with Macintosh wasn't to take him seriously.

"Why does his name come first?" asked Spencer as they joined the rest of the team and their dates.

"I was going alphabetically."

The photographer had them do the typical homecoming dance photos: arm around waist, standing arm in arm. At first, Spencer stood awkwardly next to Justice, but was surprised when Justice pulled him in closer.

"You're my date, right?" he said, in Spencer's ear. "Let's go for it. It will be fun."

It was fun at first, but Spencer grew more and more annoyed with each shot. He was too hot in his jacket, his jeans were too tight, and his feet hurt in his black leather wingtips. Also, because he was shorter, he was stuck doing the girl poses.

"Okay." The photographer clapped her hands to get their attention. "Let's do one facing each other. Ladies—and gentleman," she added, catching sight of Spencer. "Rest your hand on his chest; men, put your arm around their waist."

The team shuffled into position. Spencer put his hand on Justice's chest. Justice's heart beat slow and steady under his palm.

"Perfect," said the photographer. She raised her camera.

Justice tightened his grip on Spencer's waist, drawing him in so close that his lips brushed against the birthmark on Justice's chin.

"Looking good, everyone," said the photographer. "Now let's do a silly pose."

Spencer planned on making a funny face, when Justice lifted him up and held him in his arms as if he were carrying him over the threshold after their wedding. Spencer laughed and wrapped his arms around Justice's neck.

"Beautiful." She took several photos, the camera shutter going off. "That's a wrap."

Distantly, Spencer could hear the others clap, but he and Justice didn't move. Their eyes were level and he was so close he could count the freckles on the bridge of his nose and cheeks. He could see the delicate skin under his eyes, translucent and pale.

Finally, Spencer said, "You can put me down now."

"You can let me go now," Justice replied, not breaking his gaze.

"Come on, lovebirds!" shouted Micah, climbing into the limo.

Justice finally set him down. Spencer squeezed in next to Justice, who put an arm around the back of his seat, his hand resting on Spencer's shoulder.

Thirteen

Homecoming was already in full swing by the time they entered the gym. Music thumped in the background. The rest of the team and their dates headed to the dance floor, but Spencer hung back. He wasn't sure what the protocol was for dancing with someone who wasn't really his date. Justice touched the small of his back.

"I'm going to get punch. Want some?"

"Sure."

Spencer found a table in the back of the room. He watched the people on the dance floor. Cory was throwing shapes that nobody had ever seen before, causing people to give him a wide berth so that they wouldn't get hit by a flailing arm or leg.

He smiled as Grayson weaved his way through the tables over to where he was sitting. "Wow, you look great."

"Thanks, so do you." Grayson was wearing tailored burgundy shorts and a striped jacket.

"Do you want to dance?"

"Oh, I'm waiting for . . ." Spencer looked around for Justice and found him by the punch table talking with a girl from the soccer team who had done his hair earlier that week. She laughed and leaned forward to touch his arm.

A wave of jealously washed over Spencer. He was being ridiculous. He didn't have any claim on Justice. Justice could flirt with whoever he wanted.

He realized that Grayson was still waiting for an answer. He glanced back at Justice, who was now laughing at something the girl said.

Fine, if Justice wanted to talk with the girl, Spencer could dance with Grayson. "Sure."

He took Grayson's hand and followed him to the dance floor without looking back. This was his first homecoming since transitioning. He wasn't going to waste it moping in the corner.

For all his general awkwardness, Spencer was actually a pretty good dancer. For the first couple songs, he and Grayson bopped around together mostly just jumping to the beat. But as the music pounded, he felt himself get looser. He enjoyed the press of bodies around him, and Grayson's hands hot on his waist, running up his sides. He turned around so he was grinding on Grayson. He felt someone's eyes on him and looked up to find Justice, glaring at them from across the room.

Good.

Spencer turned back around, throwing his arms around

Grayson's neck. He spun them around so that he was still facing Justice, but when he looked up, Justice was gone.

Then Spencer felt Grayson try to squeeze his leg between Spencer's. If Grayson kept going, he would very quickly discover that Spencer did not have a certain body part that Grayson was expecting. Spencer stepped back quickly. Grayson's face was flushed, his lips were parted in surprise.

"Sorry, I—"

"It's okay," said Spencer quickly. "It's getting hot in here. I think I'm going to get some fresh air." He looked around and saw Riley in a corner wearing an amazing outfit that they had probably made themselves. "But Riley doesn't have a dance partner."

"Okay, sure," said Grayson, unable to hide his confusion.

Spencer left the gym and went out to the courtyard. It had gotten chillier and he wished he had a thicker coat. He sat on a bench, kicking a stone with his shoe. Why couldn't things be simple?

A figure appeared in front of him. "You looked like you were having fun." It was Justice. He sat on the bench next to Spencer.

"I could say the same about you."

"Who? Dagny? She goes to my church. I was saying hi while getting punch." He handed Spencer a cup.

Spencer took it. "Thanks." He was beginning to feel foolish for his outburst. He took a sip and grimaced. It was too sweet.

"They probably use a gallon of sugar in that thing," said Justice, laughing.

A grin split across Spencer's face. "You could've warned me."

"I wanted to see your expression."

Music from inside the gym trickled out. It had switched from a fast song to a slow song. Justice reached over and took the cup from Spencer's hand and placed it on the ground.

"What are you doing?" asked Spencer as Justice tugged him off the bench.

"I'm not going to let Grayson have all the fun. Come on."

Justice stepped toward Spencer, his arms out, and placed his hands on Spencer's waist. Spencer put his arms around Justice's neck.

Spencer had never slow danced with a boy before, unless he counted awkward middle school dances where boys and girls kept five feet between each other.

Justice spun him around, then pulled him back in even closer.

Spencer rested his head on Justice's shoulder. He thought about what they looked like: Justice, the good old Christian farm boy dancing with a guy.

"Are you sure you're okay with this?"

"Spencer, shut up for a second, please. I'm trying to enjoy this while I can." After a few moments, Justice's breath tickled his ear. "Will you come for dinner tomorrow? I told my parents about you saving us in the soccer game and they want to meet you."

Spencer thought about everything he knew about Justice's family. His curiosity took the edge off his apprehension. "Yeah, I'll come."

Justice pulled him tighter. They weren't really dancing anymore, just swaying in each other's arms.

Outwardly, he was calm, but inside, every neuron in his brain was firing at double time. Clearly, they were friends. But he didn't think friends held each other like this. What he knew was that he was being held by the boy he liked way more than he wanted to admit.

Making it up to the team was one thing, but Spencer knew that his parents would be a different story altogether. Sunday morning, Spencer walked into the living room, where his parents were lying on the couch. Mom was reading a book and Dad was massaging her feet. It was kind of cute in a gross way. At least it meant that Mom would be in a good mood.

Spencer sat in the armchair opposite them. "Can I talk to you both?"

Mom put down her book. "What is it, sweetie?"

"I'm sorry for lying to you about joining the team. I know it was wrong."

"We appreciate your apology," said Mom.

"But, also, I don't feel like you understand how important soccer is to me. And I want to show you something."

He hooked his laptop up to the TV and played the video he had put together. Mom gasped when a picture of him as a four-year-old smiling up at the camera holding a soccer ball appeared on the screen. His T-shirt had been so big that they'd had to tuck it into his shorts so he wouldn't trip over while playing. Mom's eyes grew teary as the video progressed. Theo's action shots showed him as he got older, his focus growing more intense but the joy in his face while playing soccer never lessening. The video ended with a picture of him and the Oakley team. Before joining he'd worried that he wouldn't fit in, but the evidence was right there that he did. He hoped his parents saw that too.

When the video was over, Mom was wiping tears from her eyes. "I can tell that this means a lot to you."

"When I'm on the team it feels like being part of something bigger than myself. I can forget about everything except playing the best that I can. On the pitch, with all the guys around me, I feel invincible."

"And I think that's what we're afraid of. You're not invincible. When we got the call last year that your school was in lockdown because of a threat to your life, we were so worried that something happened to you. Maybe we've been overprotective of you, but it's only because we love you."

"But you'll still love me next year. You can't protect me forever."

Dad touched Mom's arm. "Connie, maybe he's right. He's always going to be trans. Either we let him play, or we don't. And the team really do support him. You should've seen them when I dropped him off for homecoming—" Dad stopped, realizing he'd messed up.

"Yes?" said Mom, eyes narrowing.

"I had to let him go. Justice came to get him in a suit and everything. I took pictures. The point is, we can't hide him away forever."

"So can I see if I can rejoin the team?"

Dad took Mom's hand. "Yes, you can rejoin the team."

Spencer jumped into their arms, crushing them in a hug. While he had them on his side he sprang the next question. "Also, I know I'm grounded, but can I go to Justice's house tonight for dinner?"

Dad cuffed him gently around the ear. "I guess you remembered to follow your heart, huh?"

When Justice opened the door, the smell of freshly baked bread and roast chicken wafted over Spencer. He stepped inside to the kitchen, where children's drawings were hung up everywhere, hiding the peeling wallpaper.

A woman stood in front of the stove humming to herself.

"Spencer's here for dinner, Mama," said Justice. He stood back, almost shyly.

Mrs. Cortes brushed her hands on her apron and took one of Spencer's hands in both of hers. "I'm delighted that Justice invited you over to eat at our table. He's talked about you quite a bit."

Spencer quirked an eyebrow at Justice, wondering what he could possibly have told his parents about him.

"I haven't talked about him *that* much," mumbled Justice.

Mrs. Cortes picked up a small bell sitting on the counter and rang it. Seconds later, footsteps pounded downstairs.

Steadfast tore through the kitchen until Mrs. Cortes stopped him. "Say hello to our guest."

"Hi." He reached for the breadbasket on the counter, but Mrs. Cortes batted his hand away.

A little girl entered the room next. "Piety, will you help Steadfast lay the table, please?" asked Mrs. Cortes.

Everyone burst into action, each knowing their role. "Is there anything I can do?" Spencer asked Mrs. Cortes, wanting to be helpful.

That earned him a smile. "Here." She handed him the basket of warm rolls. "Take this to the dining room."

They moved to the table. Spencer took the seat next to Justice. Like Steadfast, Piety also had long, fair hair. Hers was braided down her back.

Just as Mrs. Cortes came back, another boy arrived at the

table. His features were closest to Justice's, but elongated, as if Justice had been stretched through a taffy machine.

"Justice, why don't you introduce your friend," Mrs. Cortes said, taking a seat.

"Oh yeah. Everyone, this is Spencer. Spencer, you already know Steadfast. That's Piety and that's Noble."

"Now, who wants to say grace?" asked Mrs. Cortes.

"I will," said Piety.

Noble groaned. "Someone else do it, please? Otherwise the food will be cold by the time we eat."

Mrs. Cortes must have agreed with Noble, though, because she said, "Thank you Piety, but Justice, why don't you lead us, since you have a guest?"

Justice reached for Spencer's hand, making him jump. Piety waited on his other side with her hand outstretched on the table, so he took it. Around him, everyone bowed their heads and closed their eyes. Spencer looked down at his own plate, his palms growing damp with sweat. He was relieved everybody had their eyes closed. Otherwise, they'd see how much he didn't belong there.

"Dear Heavenly Father," began Justice. "We thank you today and every day. We ask that you bless those who are less fortunate than ourselves and provide them with the same physical and spiritual nourishment as you have us. Also, thank you for bringing Spencer to our table to share this meal. Amen."

A chorus of amens echoed around the table, then the

room was filled with chatter of "Can you pass the chicken?" and "Would you like some gravy?"

Spencer didn't have to worry about carrying a conversation because with all the kids in Justice's family, he struggled to get any words in. He was also struck by how fast they ate. Noble went in for seconds before Spencer was halfway done with his first.

After they had finished eating, Justice nudged Spencer's shoulder with his own and whispered, "Do you want to go upstairs?"

Spencer nodded.

Photographs lined the staircase showing Justice and his siblings as they grew up.

He followed Justice into a small bedroom with a twin bed on either side.

"Sorry it's messy. I share it with Noble." Justice closed the door behind them. On Noble's side of the room there were football trophies on shelves, and a picture of him in uniform. On Justice's there was the same poster of Rafi Sisa that Spencer had on his own wall at home.

"No way, he's my favorite player."

"Mine too."

Justice picked up a guitar in the corner, sat on his bed, and started strumming.

"Will you teach me something?" asked Spencer.

"Now?"

Spencer nodded and lowered himself next to Justice on the bed.

"Sure." He passed Spencer the guitar, which settled heavily into Spencer's lap.

"Um, let's start with the C chord. Put your index finger on the first fret of the second string, put your middle finger on the second fret of the fourth string, and put your ring finger on the third fret of the fifth string."

Spencer moved his fingers to where Justice had said.

"Now strum."

Spencer strummed the guitar with his right hand. It made a dull, buzzy sound.

Justice chuckled. "Here, let me help." He shifted closer, curling his fingers around Spencer's, and pressing them down on the fretboard. "Now try," he said softly into Spencer's ear.

Spencer strummed again. The guitar vibrated against him as if it were alive and the chord reverberated around the room.

"I did it!" He twisted his head to face Justice and froze at how close they were, and the feel of Justice's hand still wrapped around his own. He stood hastily, shoving the guitar back to Justice.

He circled the room, pretending to examine books lined on a shelf willing the heat to fade from his face.

"Spencer, can you sit down? You're making me nervous."

"Sorry." Spencer wiped his sweaty palms on his legs,

suddenly very aware that they were alone. He sat next to Justice again, this time leaving lots of space between them, and sticking his hands between his thighs to stop from fidgeting.

Justice began finger-picking a melody. His head was ducked over his guitar, a lock of hair framing his face.

Then he surprised Spencer by singing. Spencer recognized it as an Elvis song. Justice was concentrating on playing the guitar, which gave Spencer the perfect opportunity to watch his fingers dancing across the strings. When he got to the chorus and sang "I can't help falling in love with you," Spencer couldn't take his eyes off Justice's face. They were sitting so close that Spencer could make out a freckle in the corner of his upper lip. Suddenly, Justice pressed his palm against the strings, muffling the sound.

"Why did you stop?" said Spencer, voice strained.

"I can't do this anymore," said Justice.

"What do you mean? Should I go?"

"No, stay." Justice put the guitar down and twisted back to face Spencer, brow furrowed. "I want to tell you something, but don't say anything until I've finished, okay?"

Spencer didn't say anything.

"You can say 'okay.'"

"I wasn't sure if you had started saying what you'd wanted to say."

Justice's mouth quirked upward. "I'm about to." His hand inched closer to Spencer's so that their pinkie fingers were touching. Spencer felt an electric shock go up his arm. "You know at homecoming when you were dancing with Grayson?"

"While you were off with Dagny, then glared at me for dancing? Yeah, I recall something like that."

"What did I just say about not talking?"

"Sorry." Spencer mimed zipping his lips.

"Well, I wasn't glaring at you. I was glaring at Grayson because he knows something about me that nobody else knows. I thought he was going to tell you before I got a chance to tell you myself."

Justice stopped talking for a moment and looked down at the floor. He took a deep breath. "Here's the thing: I'm gay."

A million thoughts rushed into Spencer's mind. At first, it didn't add up. Justice couldn't be gay. Could he? But then Spencer remembered the sleepover and how Justice didn't seem to mind him sleeping on him. Then again, the whole team was affectionate with each other. And why would Grayson know? Unless . . .

"Please say something," said Justice.

Spencer swallowed hard. "So you and Grayson are a thing, then?

"For someone so smart, you're really bad at reading signals."

"No need to be rude. If you like Grayson, you should go for it."

"Spencer! I don't like Grayson. I like *you*."

Spencer's heart leaped into his throat. "Wait, what?"

Justice didn't respond. Instead, he reached toward Spencer, pressing his palm against Spencer's cheek. His eyes closed, his dark lashes fluttering against his cheeks.

Before their lips could touch, the door opened and Noble barged in. They jumped away from each other.

"Papa just pulled in," said Noble.

"Thanks." Justice waited for the door to close, then stood up and stretched awkwardly.

Spencer felt light-headed. Had Noble seen them? And if he had, would he tell someone?

Justice wiped the back of his hand against his mouth. "We should go down," he said.

"Wait," said Spencer. Justice stopped with his hand on the doorknob. "If you're not together, why does Grayson know?"

Justice turned around slowly. "Because we sort of were together, last year." He rubbed his chin. "We were in biology and he kept getting annoyed at me winding up the teacher about evolution and stuff, so he confronted me about it and one thing led to another . . ." Justice trailed off, letting Spencer's imagination fill in the rest. Which it did, in vivid detail.

"Oh," said Spencer. Knowing that Justice had experience with a boy, and a cis boy at that . . . Spencer suddenly felt inadequate.

"It was over really quickly," said Justice.

Spencer cracked a smile. "I'm not sure that's something to brag about."

"No, not *that*. We didn't even have—I mean, our relationship, or whatever, didn't last long. You know the finals against Harlow? He broke up with me just before that because I wouldn't go public. I was pretty upset. My head wasn't in the right space before the game. That's why we lost."

"I don't think you can blame yourself for that," said Spencer. "Soccer's a team game. You win as a team, you lose as a team."

"Yeah, maybe," said Justice.

Spencer got the feeling that he didn't believe him. He heard the opening of the front door and saw Justice's shoulders tense.

"Anyway, we should go meet my dad. Ready?"

After hearing about him from Grayson, Spencer wasn't sure he was. But the tall man with a sharp jawline removing his shoes in the hallway was a bit of a letdown. He seemed normal.

Spencer stood behind Justice on the staircase as Mrs. Cortes bustled in from the kitchen. "You're home later than I thought you'd be." She took his shoes and tidied them away in the closet. "Piety, go and heat up Papa's plate."

Mr. Cortes waved his hand. "That can wait. Let me inspect the troops." Spencer watched him go through a sort of ritual: tugging one of Piety's braids, chucking Steadfast under the chin, clapping Noble on the back. Next to him, Justice's hand squeezed the banister tightly until Mr. Cortes's gaze settled on him. Justice released the banister, flexing his hand as he went down the stairs. Spencer followed behind.

Mr. Cortes grabbed the back of Justice's neck and shook him, almost as if he were a misbehaving puppy, then his eyes found Spencer, who felt his knees buckle under his intense stare.

"You're not one of mine."

"I'm Spencer." He put out his hand. Mr. Cortes's grip was so tight, Spencer felt his joints rub together.

Awareness dawned on Mr. Cortes's face. "You're the one with the killer left foot."

Spencer shrugged. "I guess?"

"No need to be modest. You made quite the impression at soccer camp. Are you thinking of coming back?"

Justice cut in before Spencer could respond. "He's pretty busy with the team."

"What a shame," said Mr. Cortes. "We'd love to share more of the Good News with you."

"The good news about what?" asked Spencer.

Mr. Cortes laughed and ruffled his hair. "You're funny."

Spencer wanted to jerk his head away. Though Mr. Cortes was smiling, it felt false, and his hand still twinged from the handshake.

"It's getting late," said Justice. "Probably time to get Spencer home."

"I'll take him," said Noble. "Give me a chance to get out of this house."

Spencer wasn't looking forward to sharing an awkward car ride alone with Noble. What would they even talk about? Luckily Justice offered to come as well. He practically shoved Spencer's shoes in his arms, pulling him out the door so fast, he barely had time to thank Mrs. Cortes for dinner. Spencer put on his shoes in the back of the car. Justice climbed onto the passenger seat while Noble fiddled with the radio dials.

A man's voice blared from the speakers. "You can call me politically incorrect, but why shouldn't we arm our own children with the word of God?"

Then the radio host said, "Surely you're not suggesting that we use children as soldiers in a religious war."

"Children are already being used by the enemy, even on our own soil. Take schools for example. You can't imagine the filth that our children are exposed to there. They're giving special privileges to homosexuals; they're allowing males to share bathrooms with females. It's disgu—"

Justice switched off the radio. Spencer privately cheered that small act of rebellion.

"I was listening to that," said Noble.

"Just leave it, okay?" said Justice. "I don't know why you listen to this crap."

"He's speaking truth," said Noble. But he kept the radio off.

Spencer swallowed back his disgust. So this was the type of crap that Justice had to listen to. No wonder he found it so hard to come out. They continued the ride in silence, except for Spencer giving Noble directions in a shaky voice.

When they pulled up to his house, Spencer was all too happy to get out of the car. Justice got out too and walked with him to his front door.

"Wait," he said, before Spencer could open it. Justice looked at the ground sheepishly. "I'm sorry about all that."

"It's okay," said Spencer.

"No, it's not."

"Yeah, it's not. But . . . I get it," said Spencer.

"Thanks for coming over."

"Thanks for inviting me. It was fun." And it actually had been up until the end.

Justice pulled Spencer into a half-armed hug, then moved back quickly. "Can we talk tomorrow?"

"Yeah, tomorrow." Spencer opened the door and went inside.

Dad's voice came from the living room, "Is that you, Spence?"

He found Dad sitting on the couch. The TV was on in the background with the volume turned low. "You're watching *Star Trek* without me? Dad, you're such a blerd."

"A what?"

"A blerd. Black nerd."

"If I'm a blerd, what does that make you?"

"I probably got it from you." Spencer collapsed on the couch next to him, resting his head on Dad's shoulder.

"It was nice of Justice's parents to give you a ride home."

"Actually, his brother drove me," said Spencer.

"And dinner was good?"

Spencer shrugged. "Yeah, but something happened on the drive back."

"What?"

Spencer lifted his head off of Dad's shoulder and told him about the radio station Noble was listening to.

"If you ever find yourself in another situation like that, give me a call and I'll come get you. No questions asked. I won't even tell Mom."

"You're not going to tell her about this, are you?" asked Spencer, his voice rising in panic.

Dad glanced around the room as if Mom might pop out from behind a bookshelf. "I don't think so. You know what she's like."

She'd probably storm over to Justice's house and conduct a sensitivity training course herself.

"What about Justice? Are you two friends, or . . . ?" Dad kept his eyes trained on the TV.

Spencer felt his cheeks grow hot. "We don't have to talk about this if you don't want to, Dad."

"What do you mean?"

"Well, last time I asked you for guy advice, you told me to talk to Mom."

Dad switched off the TV and turned to look at Spencer next to him. "I didn't tell you to talk to Mom about boy problems because I was uncomfortable talking about boys with you. It's because I don't want to give you bad advice. I mean, you know how I met your mom, right?"

Spencer had heard that story multiple times, but after he transitioned, it became even more significant to him. "Your college roommate introduced you."

"If by 'introduced,' you mean knew I had a major crush on your mom, so had his girlfriend invite her to a party where she ignored me and broke my heart, and then didn't speak to me until we had chemistry together and I was failing, so she offered to tutor me."

Spencer smiled. He loved hearing stories about his parents when they were younger. They seemed so cool. Not like now.

"And you remember my roommate's name?" asked Dad.

He smiled. This was his favorite part of the story. "Spencer."

"I love you just the way you are," said Dad, pulling him into a tight hug.

"I know."

Spencer's parents had different methods of handling his transition. When they settled on a name, Mom bought a label maker and sewed new labels in all his clothes. Dad, on the other hand, would call him by everybody else's name, including Luna, the cat, until he reached the right one. Spencer tried to be patient but soon Dad's excuse of "it's only been two weeks" turned into "it's only been six months."

By that point, Spencer had been seeing his therapist and had been referred to an endocrinologist who put him on Lupron, a hormone blocker that was injected once a month. Everybody he met saw him as a boy, so when Dad called him "she" or used his old name in public, it made for extremely awkward encounters.

The summer after he turned fourteen, Dad had taken him to New York Comic Con. They rode back to their hotel on the subway. Spencer didn't even feel out of place in his Miles Morales Spider-Man cosplay. The train car was packed, so they had to stand with Dad holding the bar in one hand and steadying Spencer with the other.

A guy sat with his legs spread over two seats, nodding along to the hip-hop beat leaking out of his earbuds. He began rapping out loud. Some of the other people in the car, including Spencer, gave him the side-eye.

The man's gaze drifted over and landed on Spencer.

"Yo, is that your son?" he said, his voice booming in the packed train.

"No, I mean, yes. This is my son." Dad squeezed Spencer's shoulder.

Spencer tried to stand taller and he widened his stance.

"He's special, isn't he?" said the guy. His stare pierced through Spencer. "You recognize that, right? You feel it in here." He pointed at his heart. "And up here." He tapped the fitted cap on his head. "Your difference may feel like a burden now, but it's actually a gift. Remember that."

Spencer's face flushed. Other people on the train were looking at them.

The guy continued, "I bet you don't even know how special he is."

They pulled into the next stop and Dad dragged Spencer out of the car even though it wasn't their time to get off. Spencer's face was hotter than the air that blasted him on the un-air-conditioned platform. Dad pushed him into the car behind it before the doors closed. "I'm sorry," he said.

Spencer wasn't exactly sure what he was apologizing for, but he never called him the wrong name or used the wrong pronoun after that. Even though his parents weren't perfect, Spencer knew they would do everything in their power to protect him and Theo. His heart ached imagining Justice in that house and knowing he didn't have that.

The next thing Spencer knew he was being lifted up by Dad and placed into bed. He must've fallen asleep while watching TV. Even though he wished he were bigger, he knew that one day, he'd miss being too big for his dad to carry and put to bed.

Fourteen

"Bad news, everyone. I presented our idea for gender-neutral bathrooms to Principal Dumas, but she said the school wouldn't consider them because it would be too expensive. We'll have to think of other ideas to put forward."

Spencer had been counting down the seconds until he'd see Justice in Music Appreciation, but Grayson's announcement brought his attention back to the QSA.

"Wait, we're just giving up?" The words left Spencer's mouth before he'd even thought them through.

"What else is there to do?" asked Grayson.

"I don't know. We could start a petition, or write an article. She'd have to at least listen to us if we got enough support."

"A petition worked last year, but I think we'd have to get a lot of signatures to make an impact," said Grayson. "Let's see what we can do."

The rest of the afternoon trickled by like cold molasses until finally the bell for seventh period rang and Spencer almost ran to Music Appreciation. Justice was already there.

He smiled when Spencer slid into the seat next to him, but Spencer noticed the dark rings below his eyes. He couldn't help but wonder if he had been the cause of Justice's sleepless night. He wanted to reach out and trace them.

Ms. Hart came into the room and announced that they'd be doing a listening and reflection exercise, which Spencer normally enjoyed since it allowed him to spend time with his thoughts and not be pressured to share them immediately. But he remembered Justice's promise that they'd talk about, well, that was the thing; he didn't know what they would be talking about.

Justice shifted so that his knee pressed against Spencer's own. Unless Spencer had hallucinated the last twenty-four hours—and he was pretty sure he hadn't—Justice had admitted that he liked him. Which left them where, exactly? His eyes flickered toward Justice, who was scribbling on a piece of paper.

Right, the listening exercise. He was supposed to be listening and writing down his reflections, but he'd missed the first song completely. He chewed the end of his eraser trying to think of something vague but specific enough to convince Ms. Hart he'd been paying attention when Justice nudged him with his elbow. He looked down at a folded piece of paper pinched between Justice's fingers. Heart hammering, Spencer leaned over to take the paper. His hand closed around it. He looked around the room to find Ms. Hart, who was busy setting up the next song, then unfolded the paper with trembling fingers. There was one sentence:

Wait five minutes, then meet me in the team room after class.

When the class finally ended, Spencer took his time packing his bag, even though he wanted nothing more than to stuff everything in it and sprint to the team room. But he was patient and waited the five minutes.

He took a steadying breath outside the door to the team room, then knocked. It opened and Justice stepped back, letting him in. He watched Justice, unsure of what to do next. Do they hug? Kiss? They settled for an awkward one-armed hug and a pat on the back.

Justice fixed his gaze on the tatty carpet. "So . . ." he began.

"Yeah," said Spencer. So far, so good.

Justice let out an exasperated groan. "This is ridiculous."

Spencer's stomach lurched like he'd missed a step. "Oh, right. I guess I'll just go, then." He turned around, ready to leave, but Justice put a hand on his shoulder.

"Wait, that's not what I meant. Look, you already know how I feel about you. And I was wondering if maybe you wanted to go out with me."

"Like on a date?"

"Well, yeah. I mean, only if you want."

Spencer nodded so vigorously, he felt like a bobblehead. "Yeah, I do."

Justice's face broke into a smile. "Really?" Justice's eyes seemed to shine in the darkness of the team room. Then his face changed. "The thing is I can't be out, out. You've met my family."

"No, yeah, I get it," said Spencer.

Justice responded by closing the space between them. Spencer tilted his head up and shut his eyes.

But then he heard the scraping of a key in the lock and sprang back. The door opened and Coach Schilling came in.

Coach Schilling jumped when he saw them. "Jiminy Christmas," he exclaimed. "What are you two doing in here?"

Spencer didn't trust his voice to speak.

Justice cleared his throat and said, "We were going over footage for districts."

Coach Schilling raised his eyebrows. "I find it usually helps to turn the projector on."

Justice coughed. "We had just finished."

Coach nodded. "Anyhow, I'm glad I caught you. I need a quick word with Harris."

Justice hesitated.

"Go on, I'll see you tomorrow," said Spencer.

Coach took off his glasses and rubbed his eyes. "I'm not sure how to say this, but I got a call from Mr. Blankenship, the league director. There seems to be an error with the sex on your birth certificate."

Cold sweat prickled Spencer's underarms. "How did they get my birth certificate?"

"We sent them at the start of the season to confirm your age. The release was part of the permission slip when you joined the team."

Right, the forms that he'd forged without really reading.

The sound of buzzing bees filled Spencer's head. He glanced toward the door, which was closed and locked from the inside. Nobody would be able to get in to help him if . . .

"Are you all right, son?" asked Coach Schilling.

Spencer gulped.

"If it's a clerical error, all we need to do is send a corrected copy."

A clerical error. He could work with that. "When would you need it by?"

"As soon as possible. You're one of my best players, but as long as your birth certificate says female, I can't let you play in league games. We'd have to forfeit."

"I'll get it fixed."

Coach Schilling ran a hand through his thinning white hair. "Good."

"Is that it?"

"Yes, thank you, Spencer."

Spencer made for the door, but Coach Schilling called out to him.

"Hang on."

Spencer looked back.

Coach Schilling opened and closed his mouth a couple times, then shook his head slightly. "I'll see you at practice tomorrow."

Spencer rushed home from school as fast as he could, bursting through the front door to find Mom in the dining room with papers spread all over the table.

"Hey sweetie, good day at school?"

He didn't answer her question. "My records at Oakley all say male, right?"

"Of course."

"What about my birth certificate?"

Mom looked up from the papers.

"We've updated your name, but it still says female."

"Why?"

"You can't amend sex on Ohio birth certificates. They don't let you."

He felt panic rising in his chest. "You mean I can never change it?" They'd done his passport and social security, so he just assumed that if it was good enough for the federal government, it would be good enough for the state of Ohio as well.

"Not until the powers that be catch up to the twenty-first century. What's this about?"

"You didn't think to tell me?"

"I didn't think you needed to know."

"But it's my birth certificate." It would have been different if it had been locked away somewhere, but it was at Oakley being seen by who knew how many people. "You should've told me!"

Mom rubbed her eyes. "There are a lot of things I don't tell you, Spencer."

"But it's *my* birth certificate! This is *my life!*"

"Fine, should I also have told you about how when Grandma sent your birthday card this year, she had written the wrong name on the envelope, so I called her and told her to send a new one? I don't keep things from you to hurt you, Spencer. I do it to protect you!"

"Well, I'm sorry that you have to put up with me as your kid." Spencer stormed up the stairs and slammed his bedroom door. She thought she was keeping things from him, but she shouldn't have bothered. He had known. All of it. They thought they were keeping their voices down, but Spencer heard the arguments, like how Dad wanted him to wait longer before starting hormones and Mom talking to well-meaning friends and relatives who had heard outdated information about the dangers of hormone blockers.

He didn't go downstairs for dinner that night, and Mom didn't come up to get him. Instead, he put on his headphones and turned on the playlist that Ms. Hart had assigned for Music Appreciation.

This week's topic was music inspired by war: protest songs,

patriotic songs, songs written during wars, songs inspired by poems written by soldiers. He let the music wash over him, soaking in the pain and sorrow that they expressed, and releasing some of his own.

The sun had gone down by the time his door opened and Mom appeared in the doorway. "Can we talk, Spence?"

Spencer removed his headphones and scooted back in bed so that he was against the headboard. Mom perched herself at the edge of his bed.

"I'm sorry," said Mom, "I shouldn't have said what I said earlier. This has been a difficult time for all of us."

Spencer didn't respond.

"I need you to meet me halfway on this, Spencer. I can't help you if you don't talk to me."

"I just hate it."

"Hate what?"

"Everything."

She considered that for a moment. "What about your brother, do you hate him?"

It was an old routine they had whenever Spencer had gotten upset. "No."

"And Luna, what about her?" she said.

Spencer smiled weakly. She could be a pain, but he loved that furball. "I guess I don't hate *everything*."

"Why all the sudden interest in your birth certificate?"

He picked at the quilt his grandma had made him. It was

blue, to replace the pink one he had before. Even though his grandma struggled with his transition, the fact that she had put in the effort to make a new quilt meant she was trying.

He debated about telling Mom about being benched. But his parents had been so hesitant to let him join the team in the first place, maybe this would be the evidence they needed to make him quit.

Mom was still watching him.

"It's nothing. Just wondering."

"You know I love you and you can tell me anything, right?"

"I know."

Mom gave his knee a final squeeze, then let go. "We ordered in tonight. There's still some pizza left downstairs if you want some."

Spencer perked up. "With pineapple and jalapeño?"

She made a face. "Pepperoni and cheese. I'm afraid my love for you doesn't go quite that far." She cupped his cheek with her palm. "We're good?"

Spencer nodded. "We're good."

Fifteen

Coach Schilling came up to Spencer in the locker room before the district game on Saturday. Spencer knew what he was going to say. He'd already checked in with him every day that week during PE.

"How are we doing on the new paperwork?" he asked.

Spencer glanced around, hoping nobody heard; everybody was going through their pre-game rituals. Justice had on his headphones and kept his eyes closed, while Macintosh crouched, then jumped as high as he could.

Spencer looked down. "It's taking longer than I expected."

"Lot of forms to fill out, huh? Well, let me know when it's done. We need you out there."

Spencer nodded, feeling bad for lying to Coach. His phone vibrated, showing a text from Mom:

We're here. Good luck today!

Spencer pressed his forehead against the cool metal locker. He'd told his parents not to come, but they insisted. He hadn't had the heart to tell them that all they'd see was him making a pretty good benchwarmer.

Coach Schilling called for the rest of the team's attention. "Listen up, I've had to make a last-minute change to the starting team. Wyatt, you're in for Harris."

"Why are you taking Twinkle Toes out?" asked Macintosh.

"It's a long season. I want to rotate players."

"Is he on the bench at least?"

"Let me worry about that. I would say 'good luck,' but—"

"Luck is for the unprepared!" everybody chorused back.

The first half of the game was a tense affair and remained at a deadlock with few chances for either team until Justice flicked the ball to Micah, who was in the box.

Micah had been doing a lot of shooting drills in practice, but Spencer still watched through his fingers. Micah weaved between a couple defenders and lined up his shot. The ball landed in the back of the net.

Spencer jumped up from the bench cheering for Micah's first goal of the season. Coach Schilling tossed his baseball cap in the air in glee.

Micah crossed his arms in the Wakanda Forever salute before the team piled on top of him.

Then the ref blew his whistle. "Offside." The score was still nil–nil.

Micah was livid. Spencer could see why. It was a tight call. Micah crowded around the referee, gesticulating angrily until the referee showed him a yellow card. Justice pulled him away before he got a red. They couldn't afford to play with ten players.

One of the Knight strikers, a slim kid with a mullet and the number 14 jersey, snaked his way behind their defenders and went one-on-one against Macintosh. Macintosh dove for the ball and clutched it in his hands, but Mullet Head didn't stop; his boots collided with Macintosh's shoulder. Spencer winced as if he could feel the impact from the bench. Macintosh rolled on the ground in pain.

Coach shouted at the referee, "You're not even going to give him a yellow for that? Come on!"

By halftime, they had managed to keep the score a draw, but as soon as Macintosh got off the pitch, he lifted his shirt to reveal a mottled bruise spreading across his shoulder. It was clear he couldn't continue. Coach told him to ice it, and then tossed a training vest to Cory.

"Start warming up."

Cory froze in horror. "Me?"

"Yes, you're our backup goalie. Now get ready to play."

The color drained from Cory's face.

"Harris, go kick him some balls."

Spencer jumped up, happy to have a chance to get off the bench and be involved in the game some way, however minor. Cory only saved about a third of his kicks. With his huge frame and quick reflexes, Cory had all the makings of a good goalie, but his brain hadn't caught up with his body yet.

Before the second half began, Coach called the team into a huddle. "We have forty-five minutes to turn this game around. I don't need to remind you what will happen if we lose. Do what you have to do."

Justice took a swig of water and spat it on the ground. "Why aren't you putting Spencer in? He's good enough. You know that."

Coach fixed Justice with a stare. "You're letting them run all over you. If you can't win because you're missing one player, then maybe you don't deserve to."

After that inspiring pep talk, the second half started. Even though the defense was playing double time, it was as if the Knights had an extra player on the pitch. Somehow, three of them got through the defensive line and faced down Cory three to one. The panic on Cory's face was visible from where Spencer sat on the bench. Mullet Head took a shot and Cory ran out of the penalty area to meet it head-on, but instead of heading it or kicking it away, he caught the ball in his hands.

Coach threw his clipboard on the ground. There was an audible gasp from the stands, then boos. Cory's eyes popped out of his head in shock. He dropped the ball as if it were on fire, but the referee already had out his red card. There they were, playing ten men without a goalie. Cory plodded off the pitch with his head down and went straight to the bus in the parking lot.

While the Knights prepared to take their penalty, Coach

Schilling called Justice to the sidelines. Spencer stood. An idea had formed while he watched the Knights build their attacks.

Justice came to the sidelines, panting. "What do we do?"

"Coach?" said Spencer.

"Not now, Harris."

"But I think I can help."

The referee blew his whistle and called Justice back onto the pitch.

"Spit it out, son," said Coach Schilling.

"It's their number fourteen," said Spencer, referring to Mullet Head. "He's the common denominator to all their attacks."

"Say it one more time, in English," said Coach.

"He's building the attacks. It all comes from him. If we can cut him off from the ball, they won't be able to get forward."

"What's the plan, Coach?" asked Justice.

The referee strode over. "If he doesn't get back on the pitch in five seconds, he's getting a yellow."

Coach rubbed his face. "Put a defender in goal and do all you can to block number fourteen."

The ref blew his whistle. Mullet Head approached the penalty spot. He brought his leg back and kicked. Then a miracle happened. The ball bounced off the crossbar. They were still in it. But they absolutely could not go to penalties.

At the next break in play, Coach took off Travis, who had

gotten a yellow card earlier, and put on a midfielder. The change would weaken their defense but would also give them a better chance at scoring a goal. The twin Oakley midfielders stuck to Mullet Head so he couldn't move without bumping into one of them. It looked like Spencer's idea was working. With Mullet Head out of the picture, the other team wasn't able to create as many chances, and Oakley kept better possession.

With five minutes left in regular time, Wyatt intercepted the ball. He thundered down the pitch with Justice behind him. The goalie dove toward him and he passed the ball across to Justice, who buried it in the back of the unguarded net. Spencer let himself cheer with the crowd, but it was far from over. It was important to keep the Knights from scoring so that they wouldn't go into penalties.

After the longest five minutes of Spencer's life, the ref blew his whistle for full time. Spencer ran onto the pitch and joined the team hug. After they let go, Justice pulled him back into another hug.

"Good call, Coach," Justice whispered in his ear.

They headed back to the bench, where Coach Schilling was talking to a man on the sidelines. Justice removed his arm from Spencer's shoulder as they got closer. The man walked up to Justice and stuck out his hand.

"Lee Johnson."

Justice shook his hand. "Justice Cortes. Nice to meet you."

Spencer's own reflection stared back at him through Lee Johnson's polarized sunglasses.

"The pleasure's all mine," said Lee Johnson. "I'm with the U.S. Youth Soccer Academy."

Justice used his jersey to wipe the sweat off his face. "I'm sorry you had to see that game."

"I'm not. I think you learn more about a player when they're losing than when they're winning." He took a card out of his pocket and gave it to Justice. "Keep in touch." He clapped him on the shoulder and walked away.

Spencer experienced a peculiar feeling of being both excited for Justice, a little proud too, and with a touch of jealousy simmering beneath the surface. He wanted to show how *he* could have cut through the Knights' defense and pull them apart.

Justice shoved his shoulder lightly. "We're still on for Monday, right?"

Monday was Indigenous People's Day and they had no school. It was also their first date. Actually, it was Spencer's first date, period, unless he counted the time in sixth grade when he went to the movies with a boy from his class and they clasped their sweaty palms together while Mom and Theo sat in the back of the theater, which he didn't.

The dark feelings disappeared and he broke into a smile. "Yeah."

. . .

On Monday, they pulled into the field used for the Fall Fest parking lot. Spencer was flooded by memories from when he was younger, mostly of being head-butted by the goats in the petting zoo and begging his parents for cotton candy only to regret it after one too many rides on the carousel. He hadn't been in years. They'd stopped going when Theo came along. He found the crowds and the noise all too much.

The ticket line spilled into the parking lot. Spencer stuffed his hands in his jean pockets and looked at the hay on the ground, unsure of what to say. It wasn't like it was the first time he'd been alone with Justice, but it was their first time officially on a date and he wasn't sure how that changed everything. Was it okay to still talk about soccer? Or now that they were dating—did one date count as dating?—was he expected to talk about other things?

Justice nudged his foot against Spencer's. "You looked like you were getting lost in there." He tapped a finger to his own temple.

Spencer nudged Justice's foot back. He realized that it didn't matter what they talked about as long as they were together.

They approached the ticket booth and Spencer reached into his pocket for the ten-dollar fee, but Justice touched his arm.

"I'll get it," he said quietly.

They spent the better part of the afternoon wandering

through the corn maze, taking cheesy pictures in the pumpkin patch, and riding on several rides that Justice assured Spencer were safe but the rusty metal bolts and fraying harnesses said otherwise. But now, they stopped to fill their stomachs with greasy festival food.

Spencer carried a funnel cake twice as big as his head in one hand and a steaming cup of apple cider in the other. He set them down on the picnic table in front of him while Justice settled on the bench next to him.

He took a bite of his funnel cake and straddled the bench to face Justice.

"Thanks for today. I'm having a lot of fun."

Justice looked at him and laughed.

"What?"

"You've got powdered sugar on your cheek."

Spencer swiped his palm across his face. When he pulled it away Justice laughed even harder.

"You've made it worse. Here." Justice picked up a napkin and reached over, wiping it across Spencer's cheek. Spencer's stomach lurched as if he were still on the Pirate Ship ride.

"There," Justice whispered, his face inches away from Spencer's.

The crash from the bumper cars and the smell of motor oil from the tractor pull faded into the distance and it was just him and Justice.

The silence was broken by a girl's voice calling out Justice's name. Justice dropped his hand and turned around.

Spencer recognized Martha from Justice's church. Justice straightened next to him.

"Martha, hi. It's good to see you," said Justice.

"You too! Is your family here?"

"No, I'm with my friend. You remember Spencer."

"Great to see you again," said Martha. Her smile seemed fake, like it was permanently etched into her face. "You're the one who goes to Oakley with Justice, right?"

Spencer nodded.

Martha lowered her voice. "I don't want to be a gossip, but I've heard about some ungodly things that happen at that school. Apparently they're considering allowing boys and girls to share the same restroom. Is that true?"

"It would be a single stall. They wouldn't use it at the same time," said Spencer.

"Even so, I'm glad I'm homeschooled."

"You do pee at home, right? I mean, that's a gender-neutral bathroom. It's exactly the same."

Justice kicked him under the table and Spencer shut up. He didn't want to push it, but he wished that Justice would jump in to support him.

Martha's face turned red, whether out of anger or embarrassment Spencer wasn't sure.

"We should get going," said Justice quickly.

"Me too. I've got to get back to the face-painting booth. I'll see you at church." She raised her hand to Spencer before heading off.

Justice stayed staring at the table for a while after she left. After a few minutes, Spencer nudged him with his shoulder. Justice flinched. "You okay?" asked Spencer.

Justice nodded, then looked up at Spencer. "It's getting late. I should get you home." He said nothing else on the way back to the parking lot. Spencer couldn't shake the feeling that he'd done something wrong. But he couldn't just let Martha spew fearmongering bullshit. After they reached the exit, the back of Justice's hand brushed against his. When it happened a second time, Spencer realized that it was on purpose. He squeezed Justice's fingers once, then let go.

"You know she's wrong, right?" Spencer said.

"About what?"

Probably everything, thought Spencer, but he didn't say that. "Oakley being ungodly. The gender-neutral bathrooms."

"I know the QSA is important to you, but my dad's sort of on edge because of it."

"The bathrooms? How does that even affect him?"

"It started last year with the dance tickets. When the pastor heard about it, he wanted my parents to pull me out, but they refused."

"Your pastor can't control your life."

Justice let out a hollow laugh. "You'd be surprised." He looked at the sky as if gathering his thoughts. "My church does a lot of good. My mom had to be on bedrest when she was pregnant with Steady and everyone made us freezer meals so we had enough to eat for months. Though, I did get a bit sick of tuna casserole. But in return, you're expected to give back. That's how it works. So my mom helps lead the women's ministry. I do soccer club. Noble does—he works with the teen group."

Justice sat on one of the hay bales surrounding the parking lot. "My family doesn't have a lot of money. We get by, sure, but there's a lot of us to feed and clothe. Luckily, my church runs a clothes drive and has a food pantry."

Justice wasn't looking at him, and Spencer felt uncomfortable thinking of all the little things he took for granted.

Justice continued, "The only thing that I have that's all mine is Oakley, and that's because I'm on a full scholarship. But I'm afraid my parents might decide it's not good for me and take me out, scholarship or not." He turned to look at Spencer. "Oakley is the only place I can be me. Do you get that?"

More than Justice knew. He couldn't bear to be the reason why Justice had to leave Oakley. "Do you think the QSA should stop?" he asked hesitantly.

"What? No, I didn't say that. I think it's great that you're standing up for what you believe in. I just need you to understand that I might not be able to be out there with you, even though I want to."

Spencer stared at the ground, embarrassed.

"Okay, now that I've spilled my guts to you, can I ask you a question?" said Justice.

Spencer nodded.

"Why has Coach benched you?"

Even though Justice had been open, Spencer wasn't ready to tell him. "He said that I lacked physicality." It wasn't a lie, exactly. But it also wasn't the truth. It was . . . a version of it.

"Seriously? Well, you just need to practice more. Here." Justice stood up from the hay bale and put down the pumpkin he'd picked in the patch. "I was going to give this to Piety, but it would be hard to get home on my bike anyway."

"What do you want me to do?" asked Spencer.

"Try to steal it from me."

Spencer got up as well and reached a leg out for the pumpkin, but Justice flicked it to his other foot. Spencer's foot hit air and he overcorrected, falling to the ground.

"You'll have to do better than that."

Spencer pulled himself up, brushing hay off his jeans. He lunged for the pumpkin again, but Justice blocked it with his body. He bounced off Justice's shoulder and fell back onto the ground.

"Are you afraid of me or something?"

"No," said Spencer. He was only somewhat lying.

Justice helped Spencer to his feet. "Then stop acting like you are. Commit to tackling me."

This time, Spencer ran forward and slid, kicking the pumpkin out from Justice's feet. He got the pumpkin, but he also managed to catch Justice and they ended up on the ground in a pile of limbs.

"That was awesome! I mean, besides the tripping part. That would probably get you a yellow card. But otherwise, it was perfect."

Spencer smiled so hard his cheeks hurt. Justice shifted so that his forearms were in the grass on either side of Spencer's head.

Spencer swallowed. "Should we go again?" He hoped Justice would say no and they could stay there forever.

A crease appeared between Justice's eyebrows and his face turned serious. "I want to try something else." He leaned down. Spencer's heart pounded faster than if he'd just played a full ninety-minute game.

Justice's face got closer to his and Spencer closed his eyes, but when he didn't feel Justice's lips, Spencer opened them again. Justice still leaned over him. Spencer had never seen him look so wide-eyed and vulnerable.

"Is this okay?" whispered Justice.

It wasn't clear if Justice was asking Spencer or himself, but he nodded anyway. Justice smiled down at him and Spencer responded by wrapping his arms around his neck and pulling his head down, crushing Justice's lips against his.

Their noses knocked together, Justice's elbow pressed into

his ribs. But then Justice shifted and they fit together like a puzzle. Justice's mouth, tasting of powdered sugar from the funnel cake, moved gently against Spencer's own. Warmth spread from his lips throughout his entire body.

Justice pulled away first and collapsed on his back in the grass next to Spencer. But before Spencer could miss his touch, he reached down and entwined their fingers together.

Justice squeezed his hand. "Just so you're clear, kissing isn't part of the tackle."

"So, you're saying I shouldn't do that in a game?"

"Not unless you're tackling me."

Spencer rolled over so he was on top of Justice and kissed him again.

Sixteen

"I want to meet him," said Aiden through Spencer's head-phones when Spencer called him that evening.

Spencer stretched back on his beanbag chair. "No, I don't think so."

"Come on. I promise I won't embarrass you. I'm just—" He pretended to sob. "Emotional. You're growing up so fast."

"Shut up," said Spencer, but he was smiling. Aiden was two years older than him and he'd already had experience with things like dating and sex. Sometimes this made Spencer feel like Aiden's annoying little brother. But most of the time, he felt like they had more in common.

"What about Friday?" said Aiden. "We could hang out then."

"I'm doing something with the team on Friday."

"Oh. How about you invite him to my gig on Saturday? Bring Riley too. That way it won't be as awkward."

Spencer twisted the headphones cord around his finger. Outside his family, Aiden was probably the person who meant more to him than anybody. If Justice was going to play a role in his life (and Spencer hoped he would), then they'd have to meet eventually. But he also felt the veil between the different parts of his life growing thinner, and he wasn't ready to be so exposed.

He cleared his throat. "There's one thing: Justice doesn't know that I'm trans." He shut his eyes tight, waiting for Aiden's response.

"Okay, got it. You know I'd never out you, right?"

"I know. But I don't know how I'm going to tell him. What if—what if he doesn't like me anymore after he finds out?" he said. It was the first time he'd said it out loud.

Aiden sighed heavily over the phone. "I'm not going to lie to you and say that it definitely won't happen. But if it does, know that I'll be there to pick up the pieces. Tell him when you're ready. Not a minute sooner. Got it?"

"Got it."

After they hung up, Spencer flung himself facedown on his bed. He was grateful to have Aiden's support, but sometimes he wished that he could just be a regular teenager and not have to worry about coming out to his boyfriend. Wait, were they boyfriends? He groaned. Why did everything have to be so complicated?

On Friday evening Spencer sat in the back seat of the Subaru, a bowl of bean dip on his lap, on the way to Macintosh's house for a team potluck.

Next to him, Theo's eyes were glued to his iPad. Mom hadn't even tried to suggest that he leave it at home since she didn't want to set off a meltdown.

"I don't see why we all have to go," grumbled Dad.

"This is a good time for us to get to know the other parents," said Mom. "Plus, we're there to support Spencer, right sweetie?"

Spencer really needed to talk to her about calling him that. But he appreciated them being there all the same.

There were already cars in the driveway when they pulled in. Spencer climbed out, balancing the bean dip in his hands. He led the way up the stone steps to the huge wooden door and rang the doorbell. It was an old-fashioned bell with a pull chain. Dad hummed the theme to *The Addams Family* under his breath and Spencer laughed while Mom shushed them.

They fought to pull themselves together as Macintosh's mom opened the door. She greeted them with Macintosh's crinkly-eyed smile.

"Come on in, I'm Judy Macintosh, Daniel's mom."

Spencer had almost forgotten that "Macintosh" wasn't in fact Macintosh's first name. He also marveled that someone so tall could be related to someone so small.

Spencer's mom reached over and shook her hand. "Connie Harris. My son Spencer's on the team with Daniel. This is my husband, Cliff, and my other son, Theo."

Mrs. Macintosh took them all in. "Welcome. The boys are in the game room downstairs," she said to Spencer.

Spencer gave Mom the dip and headed to the basement.

"Spencer, please take your brother with you," said Mom.

"But—" He loved Theo, but babysitting wasn't exactly what he had in mind tonight. He couldn't wait to see Justice again, even though they'd only said goodbye a few hours ago after school.

"Just introduce him to your friends and help him find a quiet place to watch his show."

"Come on, Theo." He took Theo's hand and headed downstairs to the basement, or "game room," as Macintosh's mom called it. On the way down, he heard Mrs. Macintosh oohing and ahing over the bean dip, which must have made Mom happy.

In the basement, Travis and Macintosh were playing FIFA on Xbox. Travis nodded at him when he came in, but Macintosh barely looked away from the game.

Spencer plonked down on one of the couches. Theo settled in next to him. The room had a large, flat-screen TV, a Ping-Pong table in one half, a foosball table in the other, and an antique-looking pinball machine. After a few minutes, the twins, Zac and Wyatt, came down. They headed over to the Ping-Pong table and began to play.

Travis paused the video game.

"Hey, what are you doing?" asked Macintosh.

"People are starting to show up. You need to be a good host," said Travis.

"You sound like my mom. You just want to stop because you're losing." But he turned off the game all the same. "Okay, we have pop in the fridge." He pointed to a mini fridge in the corner. "Food's upstairs. I've got video games, Ping-Pong, foosball. We can also—"

He stopped talking when he saw Theo on the couch. "Hi. Who are you?"

"Theo. He's my little brother," said Spencer.

Macintosh walked over to Theo and crouched down to talk to him. "What are you watching?" he asked.

Theo ignored him.

"Hey." Macintosh snapped his fingers in front of Theo's face. Theo jumped, and his wide eyes landed on Macintosh.

"Don't," started Spencer, beginning to get defensive. "He's—"

But Macintosh planted himself down next to Theo and leaned over the iPad screen. "Are you watching a movie?" he asked.

"I'm watching *Planet Earth*," said Theo.

"I love that show," said Macintosh. "You can't watch it on a tiny screen, though. Want to see it on a huge one?"

"We don't have to if you're playing video games," said Spencer. "He's fine with his iPad."

"No, we've got a movie room. Come on, I'll show you. He can watch it in there. This room gets pretty loud when the whole team is here."

Spencer and Theo followed Macintosh down the hallway and into a room that looked like a mini movie theater. It even had plush seats that reclined. Theo's eyes widened. He was in his own personal heaven.

"We can project it from the iPad," said Macintosh. "Give it here." He put out his hand. Theo held his iPad to his chest for a moment, then relented, which surprised Spencer since he usually didn't part with it unless he was forced to.

Theo wriggled into a seat while Macintosh set everything up.

"If you need anything, we'll be down the hall, okay, little man?" said Macintosh.

"Okay. Thank you," said Theo.

"No problem."

Spencer trailed after Macintosh out into the hall. "Thanks for that," said Spencer.

"For what?"

Spencer shrugged. "You know, being nice to Theo."

Macintosh cocked his head slightly in confusion. "Why wouldn't I be? He's a cute kid."

Back in the game room, Micah had arrived, and he and Macintosh started up the Xbox again. Spencer was disappointed to see that Justice still wasn't there. He turned to Macintosh, who was frowning as Micah scored a penalty against him on the screen.

"Is the whole team coming?" asked Spencer.

Macintosh glanced at him, then swore when Micah scored again. "Yeah, they should all be here soon. Why?"

"No reason. I just haven't seen Justice, that's all." Spencer hoped he sounded nonchalant. The team didn't know about them and he wanted to keep it that way.

"He's got a lot on his plate right now with stuff with his family, so he might be late."

"Oh, right." Spencer wondered what type of stuff and why Justice wouldn't have told him about it. He walked over to Zac and Wyatt at the Ping-Pong table.

They were at a deadlock in their game, each seeming to sense where the other would hit the ball, so neither of them could win. It wasn't surprising, given their connection on the pitch, but it made for some pretty boring Ping-Pong.

Spencer was so distracted by the creepy twin magic that he didn't notice Justice until he walked over to the Ping-Pong table and said, "How about me and Spencer against you two?"

Spencer's knees grew weak at the sound of Justice's voice. He turned around slowly and had to resist the urge to run into Justice's arms.

"Are you sure you want to take us on?" asked Zac.

"I think we could beat you, right Spence?"

"Definitely," said Spencer. He grabbed a paddle and took his place next to Justice. Zac's serve sent the ball to his side. He whacked it back and both Zac and Wyatt went for it.

Their paddles cracked together, and the ball bounced on the ground.

"Our point," said Justice.

They continued to play, and the twins continued to lose.

"Why isn't your twin magic working?" asked Spencer.

"First of all," said Wyatt, "it's not twin magic. We can't read each other's mind. Second of all, Zac needs to learn to stay on his side of the table. There's a white line for a reason."

"I wouldn't have to go to your side if you would go for the ball," said Zac.

"I don't go for the ball because I don't want to bump into you on *my* side of the table," said Wyatt.

"I think we're done here," said Justice, turning to Spencer. "Do you want to get food?"

"Are your parents here?" asked Spencer, bounding up the stairs behind him.

"They couldn't make it."

"Oh, right. Family stuff."

Justice froze and spun around, an unreadable expression on his face. "Who told you that?"

"No one, I mean, Macintosh said that when I asked him where you were." Spencer tried to sound casual.

Justice reached out and put a hand on Spencer's shoulder. "Were you worried about me, Spence?"

"Not anymore." Spencer pushed past him on the stairs. "Let's get food."

When he and Justice reached the table where the food was spread out, the bean dip was mostly gone. He knew his mom was worried about fitting in with these soccer moms, so he was glad that her food had been successful. Dad hovered around the food table talking to a man who Spencer assumed was Micah's dad, given that he was the only other Black kid on the team.

"There he is. Spence, come here." Spencer walked over. "Spencer, Mr. Jenkins here knows a great barbershop that's nearby, so we don't have to drive all the way to Cleveland."

"That's great. Nice to meet you, sir," said Spencer, shaking his hand.

"We were looking for a new one ever since my barber cut into my hairline," said Dad.

"You've got to check out Jimmy's," said Micah's dad. "I've never had a crooked cut there." Spencer left them to talk and made his way back to the table of food.

Spencer grabbed a plate for him and one for Theo, making sure the food didn't touch, then went downstairs. His first stop was the movie room to give Theo his plate. Theo was sitting cross-legged in the chair. He didn't even look at Spencer when he put a plate on the seat next to him. Spencer knew it would be almost impossible to get him to leave.

Back in the game room Cory was on the couch, gnawing on chicken wings. Zac and Wyatt had given up on Ping-Pong and were watching the Forest City game now playing on TV. The rest of the couch was full and Spencer looked around for a place to sit.

"Here, I saved you a seat," said Justice, scooting over so that Spencer could share his armchair.

"Thanks." Spencer squeezed in next to him and had to remind himself to breathe normally when Justice's arm pressed up against his.

The game started rough for Forest City. Within the first fifteen minutes, they conceded a goal. Everybody around Spencer erupted in groans. Spencer loved watching Forest City games. Especially since his favorite player, Rafi Sisa, played for them. Spencer wished he had a thousandth the amount of talent as Sisa. He transferred to Forest City from the Serie A in Ecuador. Sisa was smaller in build compared to other MLS players, but could pick out perfect passes from anywhere on the field.

With five minutes to go, the game was tied, and Forest City were penned in deep to their own half, another goal seeming miles away. Then their goalie punted the ball down the field. Rafi Sisa sprinted after it. All the players from the other team were deep in Forest City's half, so there was nobody to defend against Sisa. It was just him and the goalie.

"He's offside," said Travis.

"No, he was in his half when the ball was kicked, so he's onside," said Spencer.

Sisa toyed with the goalie, feinting right, then left, then

shot and scored. Spencer leaped to his feet and let Justice bundle him into a hug, which Spencer enjoyed more than he should, until something cold and wet dripped down the back of his shirt.

"Dude, I'm so sorry," said Justice. He looked it too as he held his now empty can of pop, the rest of which, he had just poured down Spencer's back.

The rest of the team laughed, but Macintosh said, "Come on, I'll lend you a shirt." Spencer followed Macintosh through his ginormous house and into what he assumed was his bedroom. Macintosh dug in his dresser and pulled out a worn, gray T-shirt, then went into the adjoining bathroom and came back with a towel.

"Thanks," said Spencer, taking the towel.

"No problem." Macintosh left the room, shutting the door behind him. Spencer removed his damp shirt and toweled off before he pulled on Macintosh's. It went down past his thighs, but the fabric was soft and it was dry. He glanced around the room. Soccer memorabilia lined the walls: medals, little plastic trophies, a pair of gloves signed by Tim Howard behind plexiglass.

He spotted a picture on the dresser of Macintosh and another boy, both in Oakley soccer uniforms, their arms around each other; laughing at the camera.

Suddenly, Spencer felt a lump in his throat. Soccer was clearly more than just a sport to Macintosh, the same way it was for Spencer. And he was so close to having it all taken away from him if he didn't figure out a way to solve the issue of his birth certificate. Coach wouldn't wait forever. He knew it was possible to fight the league's decision and win. But he couldn't see how he could fight it without coming out. And that scared him. If he came out, and if it went wrong, he had so much to lose.

Spencer jumped at a knock at the door.

"Come in," he said, expecting Macintosh. But it was Justice.

"Hey," said Spencer.

"Hey." Justice shut the door. He smirked. "Looking good."

Spencer looked down at the T-shirt he was wearing, which was practically a dress. After years of being forced into dresses, that thought came a bit too close for comfort and he hitched the shirt up, tucking it into his pants.

"What's going on?" he asked Justice.

"Just coming to check on you. And also . . ." Justice crossed the floor in three steps, wrapped his arms around Spencer, and kissed him. "Do that."

Spencer threw his arms around Justice's neck and pulled his head back, kissing him hard.

After a few seconds Justice moved away. "Your parents are here."

"So?" said Spencer, standing on tiptoe to kiss him again.

Justice stepped back, creating space. "I want to go

somewhere with you where we can be together and not have to worry."

There was such intensity in Justice's stare that Spencer's face felt on fire. Both their houses were off limits, and neither of them had a car. Besides, Justice probably wanted somewhere way out of town. Then he remembered about Aiden's gig. He'd been to a couple before. Aiden's band played at an all-ages venue in Cleveland that used to be a warehouse. Walking in, the first thing you saw was a sign that said, *No racism, no sexism, no homophobia, no transphobia, no xenophobia, only music.*

He wondered whether Justice had ever been in a majority queer space before.

"I have just the place. What are you doing tomorrow?"

Seventeen

"About tonight," said Spencer, waiting on his front steps with Justice for Aiden to pick them up. After Spencer had described Aiden to him, gauged ears, snakebites, and all, Justice thought it was better if his parents didn't see who it was he was spending time with. Spencer secretly agreed.

"You mean me meeting your best friend. No pressure or anything."

Spencer nudged him. "He'll love you. But I want to warn you, it might not be your scene exactly."

"What's that supposed to mean?"

Before Spencer could answer, Aiden pulled up in his Prius. Riley would be meeting them there.

"Ready?" asked Spencer.

"As I'll ever be."

Spencer took the front seat next to Aiden, and Justice climbed in the back. Spencer made introductions as Aiden started the car again. Aiden had a habit of drumming on the steering wheel when he was nervous, and it looked like today he was playing the drum solo from *Black Betty* by Ram

Jam (in Music Appreciation they'd done a unit about white musicians "borrowing" from Black musicians).

"So, Justice," said Aiden. "What are your intentions with Spencer?"

Spencer would have hit Aiden if he weren't driving.

"Um, I," started Justice.

"Anyone want to listen to some music?" asked Spencer. "I love music. How about you?" He switched on the radio. A country song that had gone viral was playing. Spencer was sick of it and he moved to change the station.

"No!" said Justice and Aiden at the same time.

Spencer raised his hands. "Okay, okay. Sheesh. If you want to listen to a crappy song, don't let me stop you."

"See what I have to deal with?" said Aiden. "I take Spencer under my wing, nurture him as if he were my own, and he disrespects me like this."

Justice laughed from the back seat.

"And his bad taste in music isn't the only thing you should know about him," continued Aiden.

For a split second, Spencer's heart stopped because he thought Aiden was going to tell Justice he was trans. Even though deep down he knew Aiden would never do that.

"Just wait until I tell you what he orders on his pizza," finished Aiden.

"What's that?" asked Justice, leaning forward to put his hand on the back of Spencer's seat.

"I can't say it. It's too disgusting. I'll vomit."

"Pineapples and jalapeño," said Spencer. "It's good! The sweetness of the pineapple cuts the hotness of the pepper. Don't knock it till you try it."

"I'll keep that in mind," said Justice. He squeezed Spencer's shoulder and let his hand linger there slightly longer than necessary. "So, Aiden, how long have you been playing drums?"

And just like that, any hesitation Spencer had about them meeting disappeared. They jumped into a conversation about music, which lasted until they pulled up to the venue.

The bouncer stopped them at the door.

"I'm with the band," said Aiden.

"You're good, but these two"—he gestured at Spencer and Justice—"will have to wait outside until the house opens."

"Go on," said Spencer. He and Justice joined the back of the line snaking around the building.

"What kind of music is this again?" asked Justice, glancing at the black clothes, platform shoes, and nose rings of the people ahead of them in line.

"It's like rock. With lots of screaming."

"Cool."

Spencer shivered, folding his arms tight around himself.

"Cold?" asked Justice. Before Spencer could say anything, he unzipped his own jacket and wrapped his arms around Spencer, pulling him back against his chest.

Spencer looked around and saw that there were other

couples of all genders there. Justice seemed to notice the same thing. His lips brushed the back of Spencer's neck and he said, "You know, this is the most gay people I've been around."

"How does it feel?"

Justice's lips moved against his neck and Spencer could tell he was smiling. "Sort of like being home."

Spencer sunk back deeper into Justice's chest and Justice tightened his arms around him. Spencer imagined Justice growing up, hearing that the feelings he had inside were wrong. It made his heart hurt, and he wished he could promise that Justice would never have to feel that way again, but knew it was impossible.

"When did you know you were gay?" asked Spencer.

Justice's chuckle shook Spencer's body. "When I realized that I really, really, really loved Jesus."

"This sounds like a story that I need to hear."

"I was nine years old, and we had gone to a family summer camp and they had this statue of Jesus on the cross, and I'm sorry, but he had really nice abs."

Spencer started laughing.

"It's not funny. I thought I was going to hell for thinking Jesus was hot. What about you?"

"Oh, I . . ." Spencer trailed off. Another complication of being both trans and queer. He was saved from answering when he spotted Riley and waved them over.

Spencer attempted to step out from Justice's jacket, but Justice held him tight. It felt nice being able to be like a normal couple, instead of the small touches they had to steal at school.

"Hey Riley," said Spencer. "You know Justice." Spencer had struggled with how to ensure that Justice didn't misgender Riley. He knew that Riley wasn't completely out at school and he didn't know what pronouns they wanted him to use in public.

He figured he'd avoid using pronouns at all and hope for the best when Justice said, "So, what are your pronouns?"

Spencer's jaw dropped, until he saw that instead of their usual baggy hoodie, Riley was wearing a jean jacket with an *Ask Me My Pronouns* patch stitched on the front.

"*They, them, their,*" they responded.

Spencer waited for a laugh or remark, but Justice just said, "Cool." He stepped aside so Riley could join them in line. "Wait, am I supposed to say what my pronouns are?"

Riley laughed. "You can if you want. We all have them."

"So, I guess *he, him, his*. Is that right?"

"That was perfect," said Riley.

After they chatted a few minutes, the line started moving. Once inside the venue, Spencer took Justice's hand to avoid being separated by the crush of people.

"I kind of want to stay near the back," said Spencer, mostly for Justice's sake. He'd made the mistake of going to the front before and unintentionally joined a mosh pit. He thought he'd ease Justice into it.

The three of them found a couch in the back of the room and sunk into the cushions. Justice put his arm around Spencer's shoulders, pulling him closer.

When Aiden's band came onstage, Riley got up and said that they were going to get closer. Spencer and Justice also stood to cheer as Aiden got behind the drum set and counted in the first song. The music pounded through the speakers, shaking the floor, and reverberating in Spencer's bones. As the set progressed, Justice grew more and more comfortable to the point where he even began dancing and bopping around.

He grabbed Spencer's waist and dipped his head, catching Spencer's lips in a bruising kiss. His hands trailed down Spencer's sides and he pressed their bodies together.

Spencer wished he could get so close to Justice that he couldn't tell where his body stopped and Justice's started, but he couldn't, not without Justice knowing the truth. Suddenly, the noise, the people, the heat, became too much. Spencer pulled back.

"What's wrong?" asked Justice. He wiped the back of his hand over his swollen lips.

Spencer's body was on fire. He needed fresh air. He pushed his way through the exit, ignoring Justice's voice behind him.

Out in the cold he felt feverish as his body erupted in chills. The door opened behind him and Justice burst out. He stopped a few feet away from Spencer as if afraid to come any closer.

"I feel like I did something wrong, but I don't know what I did."

"I have to tell you something."

Justice took a step closer. "What is it?"

"Wait, stay there. I don't know if you'll like it."

"Okay, I'll stay here." Justice raised his hands as if in surrender.

Muffled noises came from inside the club. There was still a bouncer at the entrance. They were far enough away that he couldn't hear their conversation but close enough to be able to step in if Spencer needed help. Spencer pressed his palms against his eyelids until he saw stars. He hated that he had to think like that. It was Justice, for fuck's sake.

"Here's the thing. I'm a guy, right?"

Justice released a breathy laugh, but his smile didn't reach his eyes. "Yeah, we're in agreement on that."

"But the thing is . . ." He trailed off, unsure of how to continue. He could say, "I was born in the wrong body" or "I was assigned female at birth," but none of those felt right to him.

"I'm a guy, but for a while I was the only one who knew that."

"I'm not following," said Justice.

"What I'm trying to say is that when I was born every-body thought I was a girl. Even I did for a few years, but then I realized that I couldn't live like a girl anymore so I transitioned. I'm transgender."

Justice stared at him blankly. "Wow, that's, um, wow."

"I get it if you don't want to date me anymore, but I wanted you to know before things went too far." Spencer slid down against the wall and put his head in his hands.

He heard Justice slide down next to him and felt him reach out and take his hand. "Thank you for telling me." He paused, squeezing Spencer's fingers. "Look, this is kind of a shock. But it doesn't change how I feel about you."

Spencer looked up at him. "It doesn't?"

"I like you for *you*. This doesn't change that."

Spencer clenched his jaw to stop his teeth from chattering.

Justice pulled him against his chest. "Come here, oth-erwise you're going to get sick and will miss the game next week and Coach will kill me."

Spencer buried his face in Justice's shoulder. "This is why I'm always on the bench. My birth certificate says female and the league won't let me play."

"Does Coach know?"

"He thinks it's an error."

"Tell him. Maybe he can help. He could talk to the league."

"But if I fight it, then everyone would know. I'm not ready for that. I came out at my old school. It didn't go well."

Justice moved back so that he could look Spencer in the eyes. "I know I'm the last person who should talk about coming out, but please think about it. Coach seems old-fashioned, but he's a good guy. He can't help you if he doesn't know."

By the end of the night Spencer's ears were ringing and his voice was hoarse from yelling and singing along to Aiden's songs.

Probably the most interesting thing that happened was introducing Aiden and Riley, who exchanged numbers. Spencer wasn't certain, but he might have seen a spark or two fly between them.

Spencer sat in the front seat of Aiden's car on the way home. He glanced back at Justice, who was snoring softly, mouth hanging open, head leaning against the window.

"He's really nice," said Aiden, voice low.

"I know." Spencer took a deep breath. "I told him."

Aiden banged the steering wheel until Spencer shushed him. "Seriously? Congrats, dude! That takes guts."

Spencer didn't answer. He was thinking about what Justice had said about telling Coach so that maybe he could play again.

"So, you wanna talk about it?" asked Aiden when they hit a red light.

"What?" asked Spencer, distracted.

"Why you're gazing out the window waiting for your husband to return from war."

Spencer sighed. "Am I a coward for not being out?"

"Dude, no. You have to do what's right for you. Sometimes existing is enough."

"You think?"

"I know." He gripped the steering wheel tighter. "I went through a phase in middle school where I didn't tell people about having two moms."

"Really?" In all the time he had known him, Aiden had always seemed so open about everything.

"Yeah, I was sick of having to answer questions about it, so it was easier to say nothing. But then after a while I felt like I was losing more by not being open about it than I would if I told people. I mean, I couldn't invite friends over. I stopped telling my moms about events at school, and then I was getting an award at the eighth-grade band concert and my parents didn't show up. That's when I realized that it wasn't worth hiding anymore. You'll know when that happens."

"I think it already has."

They were stopped at another red light and Aiden turned to look at him. "What's up?"

Spencer told him about his birth certificate and being benched.

"Wow, man, that sucks."

"I know. And the thing is, if I fight it, I know it wouldn't just help me. Think of all the other trans kids in my position but who don't have supportive parents or go to a liberal school."

"Or have an awesome best friend like me," said Aiden.

Spencer laughed. "Yeah." But it was the first time Aiden had said that he was Spencer's best friend.

"But seriously, though. I think that the more people who are out and visible, the safer it is for everyone. BUT, and this is a big but, you need to make sure that you're safe first. Physically safe, yes, but also emotionally and psychologically. Whether you come out tomorrow or in five years, or thirty years, I guarantee that the fight will still be going on in some form or another. And I promise that when you join us, we'll welcome you with open arms."

Eighteen

Grayson shared the bad news about the gender-neutral bathrooms at the QSA meeting on Monday.

"Unfortunately we only got a dozen signatures, so the bathrooms are still a no-go."

Brianna, the girl with the undercut, sighed loudly. "Finally. Now can we move on to something else that will benefit all of us?"

"Wait," said Riley. "We're giving up again?"

"What do you want me to do?" said Grayson. "I can't force people to care about gender-neutral bathrooms. Besides, we'll do something for Transgender Day of Remembrance, so it's not like we're doing nothing for trans people."

Riley's cheeks flamed red. "You don't get ally points for doing one thing for trans people when they're dead if you're not doing anything for them when they're alive."

Grayson put his hands up defensively. "Whoa, I never said that. All I'm saying is that our time could be better spent on other things. Like, what about making the front driveway a rainbow flag with chalk? It will raise awareness and photograph well for social media. Also, I kind of agree with Brianna. We spent a lot of time on this and you're the only trans student. Isn't it easier to move the ant, not the anthill?"

That was when Spencer snapped. "First of all, we're not ants, we're people. Second, Riley's not the only trans student at Oakley."

Grayson threw his arms up. "Who else is there?"

The eyes of the entire QSA was on Spencer. He felt his heart leaping out of his mouth. But he also knew that he was ready. "Me. I'm transgender too."

Spencer wished they would all stop staring or that someone would say something. Then Riley stood and wrapped him in a hug.

"Come on." Riley took Spencer's arm and led him out of the room.

"I can't believe I ever liked him. What an asshole," said Justice. They lay together on Spencer's bed after school, music blaring and the door shut.

"Grayson's all right. He ran after us and apologized. And he said he'd look into bringing in a consultant to do a transgender sensitivity training."

"It sucks about the bathroom proposal, though. Is there any chance the school will do something?"

"Not unless we get more signatures." Spencer propped himself up to look at Justice. "But hey, I don't want to talk about this anymore."

"What do you want to do?" said Justice.

Spencer moved closer to Justice. His lips worked over the tender skin where his jaw met his neck. "I've wanted to kiss you all day."

Justice's gaze dipped to Spencer's lips. "Then kiss me."

A few minutes later a knock sounded on his bedroom door. Justice and Spencer leaped apart.

Mom appeared in the doorway holding a sock so small, it was obviously Theo's. "Is this one yours? It was left in the dryer." She froze when she saw Justice furiously searching for his shirt, which had somehow ended up across the room.

Mom slammed the door shut without waiting for an answer. For a second, the only noise was her footsteps hurrying down the stairs. Then Spencer took in the mortified look on Justice's face and started laughing.

"It's not funny." Justice tugged his shirt on over his head.

"I'm sorry," said Spencer. He attempted to sober up.

"Now she thinks I'm trying to deflower you."

Spencer burst out laughing again. Justice stood.

"No, I'm sorry. Don't go." Spencer reached his arms out to pull him back.

Justice bent down and pecked Spencer on the cheek. "It's getting late. If it gets too dark, your parents will insist on giving me a ride and I don't want to be in a car with either of them right now."

"Text me when you get home," said Spencer. He heard Justice walk down the stairs and laughed at his awkward "bye" to Mom on his way out.

Spencer didn't find it as funny when Mom knocked on his door a few minutes later. "Can we come in?" she asked. Now she cared about being polite.

Dad appeared behind her looking like he'd rather be anywhere than there. Mom sat on the edge of his bed.

"Dad and I think we should go over some ground rules because we're all working without a map here."

"Why do we need a map for this?" asked Spencer.

Mom opened her bullet journal where she had made a checklist. "Does Justice know you're trans?"

"I told him last week. He's fine with it."

Mom scribbled something down in her journal. Spencer recognized her triage face: Get all the facts, leave emotions at the door.

"What about his parents?"

"No, and I don't want you telling them. Justice isn't out to his parents. They can't know."

Mom looked up from her journal. "I don't know about this whole dating thing, Spencer. Maybe I'll ask about it in the discussion group. Other parents have probably dealt with stuff like this."

Spencer put his head in his hands. "Please, Mom, I don't want the whole world talking about my love life."

"It's not the whole world, Spence, it's just Family and Friends of Transgender Kids and Teens of Northeast Ohio," said Mom, as if *that* made it better.

"I'm less worried about that, and more worried about other stuff," said Dad. "Is Justice still going to sleep over?"

"It's not like we're planning on doing anything." His face grew hot thinking about all the things he could do with Justice combined with the fact that he was discussing it with his parents.

"Spencer, it's natural for boys your age to have feelings—" started Mom.

"Mom, I've already had the sex talk. I know how it works. Besides, we weren't doing anything."

"It sure didn't look like it," said Mom.

Dad coughed. "Do I really need to be here?"

"Yes, he's your son. You need to teach him how to be responsible."

"He already knows about that, don't you?" asked Dad.

Spencer nodded.

"You know what? Since it looks like neither of you need me, I'll leave you to it." Mom pushed Dad into the room and closed the door behind him.

Dad cleared his throat, then said, "Look, Spence, I know you like Justice, but don't forget to be safe."

"Dad," said Spencer.

Dad continued. "I'm not saying don't have sex. But if and when you do, make sure you're ready and take proper precautions."

"Dad!" said Spencer. Now it was his turn to be mortified.

"I'm going to say one last thing, then we can talk about soccer. The walls in this house are paper thin."

"DAD!" Spencer covered his face with his pillow.

"That's it! We're done. How's Rafi Sisa doing at Forest City?"

After that, Mom implemented an open-door, one-foot-on-the-floor policy. Between keeping their relationship on the DL at school and the complete and utter lack of privacy at home, it wasn't long before Spencer and Justice resorted to hiding out in the old tree house in the Harrises' backyard.

It was cozy, even with the ants, and the possibility of getting tetanus from rusty nails.

Justice rested with his back against the wall, Spencer tucked between his legs. He trailed kisses down Spencer's neck and nuzzled his nose against Spencer's cheek. His nose was cold from the chill autumn air.

Spencer turned his head and let Justice kiss him. It was gentle at first. Then Justice brushed his tongue over Spencer's bottom lip.

Spencer twisted around so he was kneeling and covered Justice's lips with his. Justice buried his fingers in Spencer's hair. Then he slid his hands underneath Spencer's shirt. Spencer opened his mouth to deepen the kiss, but Justice moved his head and Spencer ended up making out with his ear.

"Wait," said Justice, "I want to make sure this is okay with you."

"It is." Spencer lifted up his shirt and pulled it all the way off. Goose bumps erupted over his shoulders. Justice pulled off his own shirt. They were skin-to-skin, chest-to-chest.

After several minutes of making out, Spencer bent his head and nipped at Justice's neck. Justice pushed him away gently and groaned. "I have to go soon. Don't get me all worked up." His voice was strained.

Spencer blushed and pulled away. He shifted again to lean against Justice's chest while Justice snaked his arm around Spencer and played a pattern on his stomach. A chill ran through Spencer. He didn't know if it was the October air or Justice's touch.

"Why aren't you coming out with the team tonight for Halloween?" he asked.

Justice's hand froze. "My family doesn't really do Halloween."

"Because it's Satan's night, or something?" He expected Justice to chuckle, but instead his body seemed to stiffen against him.

Justice took a moment before answering. "Or something."

He kissed the back of Spencer's neck again, sending tingles down his spine.

"Are you okay? You seem a little off."

Justice sighed. "Don't worry about it. I promise I'll call you later, okay?" He disentangled himself from Spencer and started down the ladder.

When Spencer could only see the top of his head, he said, "You'd tell me if something was wrong, right?"

Justice's face popped up again. He leaned forward and kissed Spencer softly. "Yes, I'd tell you. Have fun with the guys tonight."

Spencer watched him climb down the ladder and walk around to the front of the house. He pulled his shirt back on, shivering slightly as the sky grew darker and night approached.

Nineteen

Before meeting the team, Spencer had agreed to take Theo trick-or-treating. He zipped up his jacket over his flannel shirt as Theo hurtled down the stairs in khaki shorts and short-sleeve button-down.

"Aren't you going to be cold?" asked Spencer.

"No."

Spencer grabbed a sweatshirt for him anyway.

He didn't mind taking Theo and not just because it was an excuse to get free candy. Halloween had been Spencer's favorite holiday when he was younger. He loved the pumpkins, hayrides, and pillowcases stuffed full of treats. It was also the one day a year that he didn't feel like he was wearing a costume. When he was two, Mom had dressed him up as a ballerina, complete with a tutu, but the next year, he had thrown a tantrum until she'd let him be a Power Ranger. The red one, not the pink one. After that, he'd chosen his own Halloween costumes. One year it was Elmo, the next Spider-Man. But all his costumes were boy characters. Now that he had transitioned, dressing as something he wasn't didn't appeal to Spencer as much.

They walked along the lamplit streets. Other kids in costumes tore by, ringing doorbells and laughing. "What about that one?" asked Theo, pointing at a dilapidated house with junk on the porch.

"Look for a house with lights," reminded Spencer.

Theo found another one with a glowing jack-o'-lantern on the porch and cruised toward it. He rang the doorbell and a woman came to the door.

"Trick or treat," said Theo.

"And what are you dressed up as?" asked the woman with a smile.

"Crikey, I'm Steve Irwin," said Theo, in an Australian accent.

The woman looked toward Spencer, a puzzled look on her face.

"The Crocodile Hunter," Spencer explained.

"Hunting crocodiles? That sounds frightening."

"He didn't actually hunt crocodiles," said Theo, dropping the accent. "That was just his nickname. He's dead now. Can I have some candy?"

Spencer nudged him and Theo turned to look at him. "What? I said trick or treat."

The woman offered Theo a bowl and he took a piece of candy.

"And what about you?" she asked, holding the bowl up

to Spencer, who also grabbed a piece, hoping that she recognized him as the mature, responsible one and not another trick-or-treater.

As they walked back to the sidewalk, Theo said, "I think I'm done."

"We've been to one house! When I was your age, Dad had to drag me home," said Spencer.

"There's a marathon about shark attacks on Animal Planet."

"Come on, let's do a few more houses." He'd been so preoccupied with Justice, it had been a while since he'd spent any time alone with Theo. "How's school going?"

Theo shrugged. "Okay."

"Who do you hang out with?" One of Spencer's biggest worries was that Theo would have trouble making friends.

"Well, there's Charles, who stands next to me in line because his last name is Harper."

Theo's answer didn't exactly relieve his anxiety. "Right, I mean, do you have any friends?"

"Um, at recess I make fairy houses with Ella. She calls them fairy houses but really they're for insects because fairies don't exist."

Ella seemed more promising than Charles "who stands next to me in line" Harper. "Why don't you invite Ella over to play?"

"I already see her at school. Why would I want to see her at home?"

Spencer laughed and tried to turn it into a cough. "Good point, bud." He began to unwrap his candy.

"You're supposed to wait for Mom to say it's all right to eat," said Theo.

Spencer looked at the half-unwrapped candy in his hand, then down at Theo with his serious eyes and dropped the candy in the bucket.

They continued walking, dodging the other trick-or-treaters. Satisfied that Theo had at least one friend, Spencer moved on to his next worry. "What about the bus? Have you thought about trying to ride it again?"

"I don't like the bus."

"Why not?"

"It hisses."

"It what?"

"It hisses at me when I try to get on," Theo explained in a patient voice as if Spencer were an idiot.

Spencer thought back to when he rode the bus to school. Then he realized what Theo was talking about. When the bus lowered, the doors did make a hissing sound.

"So you're scared of the noise?"

Theo nodded.

"I get it."

Theo stopped walking. "You do? But you're not afraid of anything."

Spencer's heart melted. "I'm afraid of lots of things, but

sometimes you have to be brave." He pulled Theo's hand to get him to start walking again.

"Like when you stopped being my sister."

It was Spencer's turn to stop walking. "What?"

"You used to be my sister, but now you're my brother, because you were brave," said Theo simply. He skipped ahead up a candlelit path and rang the doorbell.

Spencer needed a moment to gather himself. Out of everyone in his family, it had been Theo who had the least trouble with his transition. The moment their parents explained to him that Spencer was a boy, it was like a switch flipped. Sometimes Spencer wondered if he truly understood, but clearly he did, more than anybody.

He watched from the sidewalk as Theo said "trick or treat" like they had practiced, took the treat, and said thank you. He marveled at how much Theo had grown.

Theo returned with a grin on his face. "Look what I got." He waved a rubber snake in Spencer's face.

"Cool. Hey Theo, about the bus. What if I go with you for the first day or so until you get used to it?"

Theo looked up. "Really?"

"Yeah. We can be brave together."

"Okay, I guess I'll try." Theo placed his hand in Spencer's. "I'm glad you're my big brother," said Theo.

"And I'm glad you're my little brother." He leaned down and lightly kissed the top of Theo's head.

. . .

After Spencer dropped Theo off at home, Mom drove him to Applebee's, where he joined the rest of the team. After eating too many chicken wings to count, they piled into a couple cars and hit the road for a Halloween adventure. One drawback of being the smallest person on the team was that he was stuck in the middle seat of Macintosh's SUV in between Zac and Wyatt. He had his phone out and was talking with Cory in the other car, relaying messages.

Spencer pulled his phone away from his ear and put his hand over the speaker to muffle the sound. "Cory says they want to go to the Mansfield Reformatory." The old Ohio State prison was rumored to be haunted, but boos and groans erupted from the seats around him.

"The place will be packed, if we can get tickets at all," said Macintosh.

"Don't shoot the messenger," said Spencer. "That would be a no," he said into the phone.

"Then what do you guys want to do? Micah said he's starting to feel carsick," said Cory.

Spencer repeated the message.

"He's feeling sick because he drank half a bottle of hot sauce," said Zac.

"Wait, pull over here," said Wyatt. He pointed at a plastic sign flapping in the wind that said: *True Purpose Community Church Hell House, 0.5 miles.*

"My cousin told me about this. Apparently religious nuts come together and make these. It's like a haunted house, but everything is about going to hell."

Spencer hesitated. He could think of several things about him that would make some people think he was going to hell. But he couldn't imagine that a church haunted house could be that terrifying. Funny, absurd, even, but not scary.

"How do you feel about a Hell House?" Spencer asked Cory. He waited while Cory got answers from the guys.

"We're in."

Macintosh flicked on his indicators and they trundled down the bumpy dirt road until they came to an old house with a wraparound porch. Cars were double-parked in the driveway.

They gathered outside and stared at the building.

"This looks haunted as fuck," said Micah, echoing Spencer's thoughts. They climbed the porch steps, where an unsmiling woman with gray hair pulled into a tight bun took five dollars each in exchange for a ticket with the words *Matthew 13:49–50* written on the back.

The front door led into a small, unlit hallway. There was a staircase straight ahead. Glow-in-the-dark arrows were stuck to the floor, showing the way. They followed the signs to the first room. It was dimly lit, but Spencer could tell that it was made up to look like a hospital ward, complete with the sound of beeping monitors and a motorized bed. A girl lay in the bed with her knees bent and legs raised. A blanket covered her bottom half.

She opened her mouth and screeched like a banshee. Wyatt jumped back, stepping on Zac's foot, and Zac let out a yelp. Spencer laughed at Zac, but then flinched himself when someone dressed in scrubs and a red devil mask sprung out from the shadows.

The doctor messed around under the blanket. He pulled out a doll covered in blood and held it up to the crowd as more blood squirted out from under the blanket. The girl convulsed for a few seconds, then "died."

"That was strange," said Cory. The team exchanged looks. Spencer half hoped someone would suggest leaving, but they moved on to the next room.

Inside was another bed, but this time it was a young couple debating whether they were ready to have sex. In the end, the boy pressured the girl into agreeing. It was kind of funny because "having sex" meant that they held hands and got under the covers together. But then it turned out that the guy had an STD and the girl died.

"Oh, so that's how you have sex," said Micah. A mother of two preteens who had also joined the tour shot him a dirty look.

"I wonder what's next," said Cory as they left the room. Spencer noticed Macintosh's forehead was creased in a frown.

"I bet somebody dies," said Spencer. He didn't want to

know what his fate was as a queer trans guy, but he followed the team to the next room.

The wall was covered with a backdrop to look like a locker room and two guys were sitting on a bench kissing. It was clear from the badly done makeup that one of the guys was actually a girl in drag.

Two more characters came onstage. A devil, complete with red robes, horns, and red face paint, and an angel wearing white robes and a halo.

The devil told the boys that being gay was okay, while the angel told them they would go to hell unless they repented. In the end, one of the boys repented while the other one chose the gay lifestyle. Spencer was pretty sure what would happen next.

He'd seen enough. "I'll meet you guys back at the car." He thought that maybe he'd be able to laugh at the absurdity of it all, but in reality he felt disgusted. They might have been silly scenes, but they had real-life consequences, and he hated that his five dollars was going to people who believed such crap.

He was so upset that he didn't see the person coming around the corner until it was too late.

They collided into each other. The other person dropped the bucket they were holding and a warm, sticky liquid covered Spencer.

He looked down to see that he was covered in blood. Fake blood, he realized.

"I'm so sorry. Let me—" The person he had collided with broke off. "Spence?"

It was Justice.

"What are you doing here?" asked Justice.

"I could say the same to you." It was as if someone trampled over his heart wearing soccer boots. Two hours ago they had been making out in Spencer's tree house. He didn't understand how Justice, *his* Justice, could be involved in something like this. He couldn't deal with it, not tonight. He stumbled backward.

"Spencer, wait!"

Spencer ignored him. His shoes stuck to the wood floor as he ran down the hallway.

Justice caught up to him before he reached the front door and grabbed his arm. "Will you let me talk?" He looked desperate.

He wanted to talk? Spencer would talk. "How can you make out with me one minute and then do this the next?"

"Keep your voice down. Come here." Justice pushed him into what turned out to be the bathroom. "You know I don't believe in any of this, right?"

Spencer crossed his arms. "I don't know what to believe."

A look of hurt flashed across Justice's face. "Come on, Spencer. You know me."

"The Justice I know wouldn't be involved in something like this."

"I didn't have a choice."

White-hot rage boiled up in Spencer. "You always have a choice."

"It was this or leaving Oakley. My dad thought that getting more involved in the church would help counteract some of what he saw as bad influences there."

Spencer momentarily softened, then grew angry again. He narrowed his eyes. "So as long as you get what you want out of it, it's okay to spout this abusive bullshit?"

"I didn't say that."

"You want to know why I don't want people knowing I'm trans? It's because of people like your family."

Justice recoiled like Spencer had slapped him. "How do you think I feel? This is my life." He braced himself against the sink. "Not everyone has supportive parents like you do," he said bitterly. "My family takes His word literally. Steadfast is only eight. One day we were at the park and my mom told him to stay in the playground, but he didn't listen and wandered off. It took us an hour to find him. The next Sunday he got saved. I asked why he decided to get saved. You know what he told me?" Justice smiled sadly. "He said that when he couldn't find us, he thought we had all been Raptured and he didn't want to be left behind."

"That's fucked up," said Spencer.

"Tell me something I don't already know." Justice rubbed his face. "Spencer, I don't think I can do this."

Now it was Spencer's turn to falter. "What do you mean?"

"If my parents found out . . ."

"What are you saying? Are we breaking up?" He began to shiver, the fake blood growing cold against his skin. He didn't wait for an answer. Spencer opened the bathroom door, ignoring Justice's plea to wait. But someone was on the other side.

It was Martha. Spencer didn't know how much she had heard, but at that point, he didn't care.

After Macintosh dropped him off, Spencer showered and changed into his pajamas, then went back downstairs to the living room, where his parents watched TV. Theo knelt in front of the coffee table sorting his candy.

"Ready to talk?" asked Mom.

Apparently "no questions asked" didn't apply when you came home crying and covered in blood, even if it was fake.

He squished himself between them on the couch. "We broke up."

"Oh, sweetie," Mom pulled him against her into a hug and rocked him. "I'm sorry."

"You know," said Dad. "Maybe this is a good thing. You'll have less distractions at practice and get more game time."

Spencer let out a snort. "Yeah, that's not going to happen."

"What do you mean?"

Spencer's nerves were rubbed raw, but he was sick of keeping secrets. He'd tried that and it had gotten him nowhere. "I've been benched."

"What?" said Dad. "You're one of the best players on the team. I've seen you at practice. The other day you were pressing so high up the pitch that your goalie was sitting on the ground making daisy chains."

"He was looking for four-leaf clovers," said Spencer. "Cory's grandpa said that if he found one, he'd give him a thousand dollars."

"Is his grandpa a leprechaun?" interrupted Theo.

"I thought fairies weren't real," said Spencer.

"Leprechauns aren't fairies," argued Theo.

Dad broke in, "His grandpa could be a goddamn Keebler Elf for all I care. Why isn't Coach Schilling letting you play?"

What Spencer wanted to do was debate whether leprechauns and elves were both part of the fey family, but judging by the vein popping up on Dad's forehead, that discussion would have to wait.

"It's not Coach. The league won't let me play because my birth certificate says female." There, he'd said it.

"Why didn't you tell us earlier? We could've done something," said Mom.

"Like what? You said yourself that we can't change it. Besides, you didn't even want me to join the team in the first place. I thought you'd make me quit."

"That's different," said Dad. "Yes, Mom and I were worried about you joining the team, but this is big. We're talking about your civil rights."

"It's not that I haven't thought about it," said Spencer. "But if I come out and fight, it would put all of us under a microscope."

Mom pulled him closer. "When you first came out, Dad and I had to make a lot of the decisions for you. But you're older now and this has to be your choice. When you're ready to make a decision, just know that we'll be here to support you either way. Who was that wrestler in Texas?"

"Mack Beggs. He still had to wrestle against girls, though," said Spencer. "And I don't think I'm brave enough to deal with the hate he got."

Theo came over and dumped a handful of candy in Spencer's lap. "We'll be brave together. Right?"

Spencer hugged Theo fiercely. Theo, who wasn't a huge fan of hugs, put up with it for a couple seconds, then patted Spencer on the head until he let him go. "Thanks, Theo."

Dad picked up a candy. "Smarties? No idea how you can eat those bits of chalk."

Spencer laughed, despite himself. He stifled a yawn, suddenly aware of how tired he was. "Save them for me. I'm going to go to bed now."

He lay in bed for a while staring at the ceiling thinking over his options. Even if he couldn't play, he still had friends on the team. All of that could change if he came out. And even if he did come out, he had no guarantee of winning; then where would he be?

Before turning off the light he took out his phone and deleted Justice from his contacts.

Twenty

Unfortunately, there was no way Spencer could delete Justice from real life.

At the last practice before the semifinals, Spencer had the ball at his feet and pounded down the pitch toward goal, where Macintosh crouched, tracking him with his eyes. Micah was behind and Justice was up ahead. Spencer slowed down and did a nutmeg, threading the ball through Travis's open legs, then picking it up again at the other side of him. He glanced up. Justice was unmarked near the goal. Instead of passing to him, Spencer sent the ball backward to Micah, but his shot went wide.

The piercing shriek of Coach Schilling's whistle made Spencer cover his ears.

"What in the hell was that, Harris?"

Spencer doubled over to catch his breath. "Sorry, Coach."

Coach Schilling marched onto the field. "Harris, how many points are in a triangle?"

"What?" asked Spencer.

"I said how many goddamn points are in a goddamn triangle?"

"Three," said Spencer, confused.

"Eureka, he does have a brain!" shouted Coach Schilling. "There are three points in a triangle, just like there were three players in that attack." He counted off on his fingers. "There's you, Micah, and Justice. So why in tarnation didn't you pass to Justice when he was open?"

Spencer focused on the muddy pitch. "I didn't see him, Coach."

"You didn't see him?"

Spencer felt the tips of his ears go red.

"You know, I'm not surprised." Coach rounded on Justice. "Why didn't you call for the ball when you were open? It was like you didn't want him to pass to you."

"Sorry, Coach," Justice mumbled.

"Don't apologize to me. Apologize to your team when we lose the semifinals on Saturday."

"Is Spencer even going to play?" asked Cory.

"That's my business. But, hey: If you care so much about him, you can help Spencer pick up the cones and balls before going in."

Spencer wiped the sweat off his face with his T-shirt and stood with his hands on his hips.

Cory tossed a bag at him. "You get the balls, I'll get the cones."

Spencer circled the field gathering the balls.

"You want my advice?" asked Cory.

"Not really," said Spencer.

Cory ignored him. "Buy Coach Schilling a subscription box of Omaha steaks and apologize for whatever you did."

"What are you talking about?"

"Dude, Schilling loved you at the beginning of the season, but now he's benched you for apparently no reason. You must've pissed him off somehow. Just apologize."

"Why do you care?" he snapped back. "I thought you'd be happy to have some company on the bench." He regretted it the moment the words left his lips.

Cory dropped his bag of cones and walked away.

"Cory, wait. I'm sorry, man." But it was too late. Cory stormed inside, letting the door slam shut behind him.

Spencer put his hands over his face and yelled. He found a ball and kicked it toward goal in frustration. It bounced off the crossbar. He got another one and did it again. This time the ball went in the net. He didn't know how long he stayed out there, kicking ball after ball toward goal, but eventually he heard footsteps behind him.

"How about we make this a little harder for you, Twinkle Toes." Macintosh pulled on his gloves and got in between the sticks.

Spencer was grateful for the company and further distraction. He kicked the ball toward the center of the net. Macintosh caught it and rolled it back to him. Spencer tried again, this time aiming the ball into the corner. Macintosh dove but missed. He wiped mud off the ball before kicking it back to Spencer.

They kept going until the sun dipped down below the horizon and Spencer's shirt clung to his back. At last he bent over, hands on his knees, exhausted.

Macintosh left the goalposts and put a hand on his back. "Feel better?"

Spencer nodded. Distilling the game to its simplest form of foot, ball, net had cleared his mind and numbed his emotions.

"I probably should've warned you not to get involved with your teammates."

Spencer coughed, choking on his spit in surprise. "I don't know what you're talking about."

"Your little thing with Cortes. What? You think nobody noticed?"

Spencer shrugged.

"I was happy for him. For both of you. But dating your teammates can get messy. I should know."

Spencer looked at him, shocked.

"I had a thing with a striker on the team last year."

"A sex thing?" blurted out Spencer.

Macintosh smirked. "I mean, we were going out."

"And the rest of the team was all right with it? They didn't mind you two dating?"

"Not as long as we kept winning."

"Are you still together?"

"Me and Nate? Nah, he's a freshman at OSU now."

"If you're gay—" began Spencer.

"Actually, I'm bi."

"Oh, sorry. If you're bi, how come you're not pissed at Justice for the Hell House? I mean, you can't think that was right."

They moved to the bleachers. The cold metal stung Spencer's skin.

"I know it wasn't right. Justice knows it wasn't right. But I don't think he had much choice. He talked to me about it afterwards. Originally he was supposed to play the devil in the gay scene, but he told his brother that he wouldn't do it, so they gave him a support job instead. I get that it might not mean much to you, but for Justice even standing up to his brother that much was a big deal."

Spencer recalled the uncomfortable car ride home with Noble, and Martha's look of disgust when she talked about the gender-neutral bathrooms. If these were the kids Justice hung around, Spencer couldn't imagine what the adults were like. His pastor. His parents. The people who Justice should be able to trust. Instead he had to keep part of himself, a really, truly, wonderful part, hidden

"I think I get that, but I don't understand why he didn't tell *me* about it," said Spencer.

Macintosh arched an eyebrow. "You ever keep a secret before?" he asked.

Spencer nodded.

"Then you know why." He placed a hand on Spencer's shoulder. "Anyway, it's getting late. Let's pack it in."

To Spencer's annoyance, the rest of the team was still in the team room when he and Macintosh arrived. Coach Schilling was reviewing last-minute plays for the semifinals.

"Oh good, you're here. I was just about to go over the starting team."

Spencer took a seat in the back of the room. He let his mind wander while Coach announced the team and formation. It didn't matter. It wasn't like he was going to play anyway. He wondered what he was even doing there at all. The team didn't need him sitting on the bench.

The whole reason he didn't want to come out was because he was afraid of what people would think of him. But the team already thought he was in Coach's bad books. Maybe if they knew why Coach wouldn't put him in, they'd understand, be sympathetic even.

Aiden's words about coming out came to mind. He had come out when the cost of not doing so outweighed the risk. That afternoon, Spencer felt the balance tip in that direction.

Without realizing it, he was on his feet. Coach broke off.

"I need to say something."

"I'm sort of busy here," said Coach.

"This is important." He looked around at the team. "You've probably noticed that I'm not playing as much anymore."

"Or at all," said Cory.

Spencer ignored him. "Coach did bench me, but he had no choice. The league won't let me play because my birth certificate says I'm female."

The room fell completely silent.

"And the reason it says that is because I'm transgender."

They all stared at him like he'd suggested that he should take over in goal for Macintosh. He looked down at the ground.

"I thought you guys should know," he finished weakly. Before anyone could respond, he rushed out the door and retreated to the locker room, where he sunk down on a bench, his head in his hands. He couldn't believe he'd just done that. Now he waited to see if it was worth it.

He didn't have to wait long. Cory came in first. He patted Spencer on the shoulder. "Hey, I'm sorry about earlier."

Spencer looked up and gave him a watery smile. "I'm sorry too. I was a jerk."

The rest of the team trickled in behind Cory. Macintosh kneeled in front of him. "Hey, Twinkle Toes. We all have your back. If anybody has a problem with you, they have a problem with us. You're our brother." He put out his fist and Spencer bumped it with his own.

The rest of the guys crowded around him. Some of them messed up his hair, gave him a fist bump, or slapped him on the shoulder. But they all told him that they had his back.

The only one missing was Justice. Spencer tried not to let it bother him.

Once the team cleared out, Coach sat down on the bench next to him. "You know, my son was a very talented athlete, much like yourself."

Spencer thought back to the little boy in the photograph on Coach's desk. He'd probably be in his twenties now. Spencer wondered if he was still playing.

"His sport was baseball. He played on the school team and a select travel team. Then in the summer, he'd do camps and clinics. Sometimes my wife and I worried that we were pushing him too hard. But when he was seven, he threw a ball from the outfield to first base and one of the dads in the crowd said, 'Damn, I wish I had an arm like that.'" He chuckled softly. "This was a grown man talking about a seven-year-old. Of course we had to nurture his talent. Then in high school, he tore his rotator cuff, but he didn't tell us at first because he didn't want to disappoint anyone."

Spencer could sympathize. He knew what it was like to fear losing what you cared about most.

Coach Schilling continued, "Soon, he could barely play and it became clear that he needed surgery. Even with surgery, he suffered from chronic pain, and he became addicted to painkillers." He broke off, his voice growing gruffer. It sounded like he'd been wanting to tell this story to someone, but Spencer didn't understand why he had chosen him.

"When he could no longer get a prescription, he turned to heroin. He overdosed days before his twentieth birthday."

Spencer was too shocked to respond. He couldn't imagine the pain Coach must have felt losing his son.

Coach Schilling wiped his eyes. "For a long time I blamed him for not telling us he had a problem starting from his first injury. I thought all of this could've been avoided if he'd just opened up. But then I realized that I didn't make it easy for him. I never asked how he was doing, how he was feeling, if he still wanted to play, or what I could do to help him."

Coach Schilling twisted his body so he and Spencer were eye to eye. "So I want to apologize to you. That day when I asked about your birth certificate, I admit, I suspected that it was something other than a clerical error. But I should've let you know that you were safe with me, and for that, I'm sorry." He paused, then tapped Spencer on the knee. "The question now is what do you want to do about this and how can I help?"

Spencer always assumed that coming out was a one-way thing, that the responsibility fell on him, and him alone. But Coach's story made him reconsider. Just because the onus always fell on trans and queer people, didn't mean it *should*. He realized Coach Schilling was waiting for an answer to his question. Now that the team knew, maybe he could fight the league's rule. Except . . . "The season's almost over."

"True. But what about next year? The year after that? You can't sit on the bench forever, Spencer. Whatever you decide to do I want you to know that you have my full support."

All of Spencer's reasons for not fighting the league swirled around his head, but Coach was right: He couldn't wait on the sidelines, and he shouldn't have to. Plus, if there was a chance that he could help another trans kid, shouldn't he take it? He knew what he had to do next. As soon as he got home, he called Aiden.

"How's this for a pitch: 'Transgender teen denied the right to play soccer for progressive private school.'"

He pulled the phone away from his ear when Aiden shrieked. "Are you giving me an exclusive?"

"Yes, let's do this."

Twenty-one

On Wednesday, Aiden picked him up after school and drove them to what looked like a run-down house with boards on its windows.

"I know it's not much."

Spencer spotted a pride flag hanging in an upstairs window. "It looks perfect."

There was a sign on the door that said *Bell broken. Knock loudly,* but Aiden pulled out a key and let them in.

Inside was a cozy office space filled with mismatched chairs and a comfy, worn couch. Different-colored pride flags covered the walls.

A white man in a cardigan looked up from behind his desk. "You must be Spencer." He got up and walked past a large dog who opened an eye when he stepped over her on the carpet, before rolling over with a grunt. "That's Lola, the worst guard dog ever, and I'm Laurence." He put out a hand to shake Spencer's.

"I was really pleased when Aiden pitched this story and said you'd let us interview you. You can take a seat here." He gestured to the couch, which sunk down when Spencer and Aiden sat. "Do you mind if we record this so I don't have to take notes?"

"Go ahead," said Spencer.

Laurence set up his phone to record on the upside-down crates that stood in as a coffee table.

"First, let me just say that I think what you're doing is amazing."

Spencer shrugged it off. He hadn't done anything yet.

"Second, if I ask you anything that makes you feel uncomfortable, feel free to tell me to fuck off."

Spencer laughed.

"He's serious," said Aiden. "I tell him that all the time."

Laurence ignored Aiden. "So, tell me, what do you hope to accomplish by doing this?"

Spencer ran a fingertip along the corduroy couch cushions. "I want to play, first of all. But also I've had it pretty easy, all things considered. And I feel like if I do this, then I'll make it easier for other trans kids who might not have the support of their family and friends like I do."

"That's really neat," said Laurence. "After I came out, I had a couple awful years where I was misgendered all the time, threatened in bathrooms, you name it. So, when I passed, it was like I could breathe again without worrying. For a while, I cut myself off from all things trans. But I found that I missed it. There were things I couldn't talk about with my cis friends, and they would sometimes say something transphobic and I would laugh along, and I realized I was part of the problem.

"But I guarantee that if I had someone like you when I was growing up, my life would've gone so differently. I love that trans youth have people like you and Aiden to look up to. Hell, I look up to you both, and I'm thirty-five."

Spencer smiled back, slightly embarrassed, but pleased with the compliment. Any lingering concern melted away.

They ended up talking for almost an hour. At the end, Laurence shook his hand. "Expect it to go live in a couple days. And good luck, Spencer."

The story broke on Friday, but Spencer didn't realize how much momentum it had gained until he arrived for the semi-finals the next day. Satellite trucks lined the Oakley parking lot and reporters huddled on the sidelines with microphones and cameras.

In the locker room before the game, Coach called for silence. "Let's try to block out any distractions. We've prepared hard for this game. Now let's give them a show." His gaze flickered around the room. "Hang on, has anybody seen Justice?"

Spencer looked around. Justice wasn't there.

"He's not answering his phone," said Dylan.

"Maybe he's running late."

When Justice didn't show up by warm-ups, Coach Schilling replaced him in the lineup.

Anxiety began spreading through Spencer, and not

because of the game. It wasn't like Justice to miss a match. He couldn't help but feel like it was his fault somehow.

As Spencer waited in line to shake hands with the other team, he heard a couple of the Wanderers players talking.

"Who do you think used to be a girl?"

"Probably number sixteen."

"It would be so weird having to share a locker room with her."

"Him, you mean."

"Whatever. I'm pretty sure he doesn't have a dick."

When it was Spencer's turn to shake that player's hand, he made sure to squeeze it as tight as he possibly could and was satisfied to see him flexing it afterward.

When they'd finished handshakes, Spencer took his seat on the bench next to Cory. He looked up into the stands to see if he could spot his family. He'd told them they didn't have to come since he wasn't playing, but Dad had said he wanted to support the team. Spencer suspected they really came because they were worried about his safety. He found Theo in his ear protectors holding a homemade sign with his name on it. He caught Theo's eye and waved. Theo waved back. Seeing them there helped calm his jitters.

Spencer was pulled back to the game when Cory nudged him.

"What?"

Cory pointed at the field excitedly. Spencer followed his finger. The team was in position for kickoff and every player wore an armband in the light blue, pink, and white stripes of the transgender flag.

Seventy minutes in, the team was down a goal.

Wyatt had the ball and was looking for another player to pass to when a Wanderers defender tackled him from behind, stabbing his calf with the spikes of his boot.

Wyatt fell to the ground clutching his leg. The referee knelt next to him. They exchanged a few words that Spencer couldn't make out, then the referee signaled for the medical staff. They helped Wyatt to his feet, and he limped off the pitch to polite applause, blood blooming on his sock where the boot studs pierced his skin.

Coach Schilling ripped off his hoodigan and threw it on the ground. The defender only got a yellow, with what could have easily been a red card challenge.

After the medics wrapped his calf with an ice pack, Wyatt hobbled back to the bench and put his head in his hands. Spencer wanted to look away from the train wreck of a game as well, but he couldn't. The Wanderers scored again and he groaned.

Coach tugged at his hair, dangerously close to pulling out the remaining wispy strands. He pinched the bridge of his nose with his fingers. After a second, he looked at Spencer with clear eyes. He reached into the cardboard box by the bench and tossed him a bib. "Harris, start warming up."

Spencer stared at the bib dumfounded. He must have heard wrong. "But then we forfeit."

"I know that. But I'd rather win and forfeit than keep one of my best players on the bench because of some asinine rule."

Spencer pulled off his sweatshirt, barely registering Coach's compliment. He tugged a training bib over his head and began to stretch. Then he jogged up the length of the pitch, analyzing the game. A few minutes later, after a pause in play, Coach told the fourth official that he was putting Spencer in.

From the bench, Spencer had noticed that every chance the other team got was through the left side of the pitch. First, they'd need to shut that down. Then they needed to take advantage of the space their opponents left behind as they came to attack.

He called the team over to him and told them his plan.

"Give them *more* possession? Why don't we just take a seat in the middle of the field and let them score?" scoffed Micah.

"We don't have the width without Justice. The only way we'll beat them is on the counterattack. We have to force them offside and find space through the back."

A few of them shook their heads like he was delusional, but they agreed to Spencer's plan. For the next few minutes, they played a patient game, shutting down any opportunity the Wanderers had of scoring. All they needed was one chance.

It came when Travis performed a perfect slide tackle,

sending the ball spinning across the pitch. Spencer got it and sent it to Micah, who was onside with tons of space. If he could, Spencer would have crossed his fingers, hands, arms, toes, whatever, willing Micah to hit his target.

Micah took the shot and the ball curled into the top of the net.

The team rushed both Spencer and Micah and he collapsed under the bodies of his cheering teammates, but it wasn't over. They had a game to win. Once the team understood the plan, it was almost easy. They hung back, allowing the Wanderers to have the ball, but prevented them from attacking the goal. A second chance at a goal came through Travis again. He intercepted one of the backward passes, sending the ball to Spencer, who buried it in the back of the net.

They were tied with five minutes to go and both teams were on edge. There was a scary moment when an Oakley defender lost the ball in front of the goal. Luckily, Macintosh was there to catch it. He tossed it to Spencer, who controlled it, then ran forward up the pitch. He didn't flinch as a defender attempted to shove him off the ball. Instead, he snaked it through to Micah, who managed to deflect it off a Wanderer player and into the net for a brace.

When the referee blew his whistle for full time, Spencer collapsed on the field, chest heaving. Based on the sound of gasping and heavy breathing around him, the rest of the team was equally drained. He stayed like that until a small hand rested on his shoulder.

Theo frowned down at him. "You won. Why are you sad?"

Spencer pulled Theo to him. Yes, they had won, but it didn't matter. They were disqualified from the tournament.

Spencer emerged from the locker room to find a camera in his face. A woman approached him holding a microphone. "Jeannette Perkins from channel seventeen. So nice to meet you." She flashed her shark-tooth-like smile at him. "I'd love to ask you a few questions about the game, if that's okay?"

This was his moment. If he didn't want the team's disqualification to be for nothing, he had to act now.

The segment aired on channel 17 later that night. He sat on the couch next to Theo and watched as he appeared on screen juggling a ball from knee to foot, to chest and back again.

Jeannette Perkins's voice came from the TV. "This is Spencer. He's a lot like other fifteen-year-olds. He goes to school, he has a loving family, he's a star player on his high school soccer team." The video cut to a clip of him scoring the goal in the game that afternoon.

"But Spencer is different. Though he identifies as a boy, Spencer was born a girl."

Spencer winced at the outdated phrase. Then Mom and Dad were on the screen sitting in the bleachers. "I was so excited to have a little girl to dress up, but by about two he refused to wear the dresses I put him in."

"When did you realize that there was something different about Spencer?" asked Jeannette, leaning in closer to Mom.

"From an early age it was clear that he wasn't comfortable doing what other girls were doing, but I never thought he was transgender. We all thought he was a tomboy. It wasn't until puberty that I truly understood how unhappy he was."

Spencer covered his face in his hands. Nobody should have to listen to their mom talk about them going through puberty on TV.

Screen Mom continued, "He went through a tough time and finally he was like, 'Mom, I can't do this. I can't be a girl. I'm a boy.'"

"And how did you feel?" prompted Jeannette.

"A range of emotions. Scared, confused, guilty that I didn't know this about my own child. Upset that he felt like he had to hide it from me. But I got support. That's one thing I'll say to parents of transgender or gender-nonconforming children. There's tons of support out there." She looked straight at the camera when she said this.

It cut to a clip of Spencer passing the ball around with the team. They had all stayed behind after the game to film and do one-on-one interviews.

Back on the screen another voiceover began. "After a series of bullying incidents, and even threats of violence, Spencer and his family decided to switch to a private high school for a fresh start. Spencer joined the soccer team and quickly made friends."

Macintosh's goofy face appeared on the screen. When shooting, they'd had to adjust the camera because he was too tall for the frame. "When I first met Spencer he tried to take my head off with a ball. That's when I knew we needed him on the team."

Jeannette's voiceover continued over another clip of practice. "But then his coach got the news that Spencer couldn't play in tournament games because of one small word."

Spencer was on the screen again holding a copy of his birth certificate from his file in the Oakley office. Most of the information was blurred out but the *FEMALE* next to *sex* was visible.

Spencer watched himself on the screen talking to Jeannette.

"In some states, trans people can change their gender marker, but Ohio doesn't let you. The league goes by what's on your birth certificate and not common sense, so I got benched during games."

Then Coach Schilling was on camera. He had brushed off the styling crew who attempted to pat down his wispy hair.

"You allowed Spencer to play today, even though it led to your team's disqualification. Why?" asked Jeannette.

"Spencer is without a doubt one of the best players I've ever coached. He's got natural instincts for the game, something that can't be taught. The league's decision to ban him is disgraceful and I'm proud to stand behind him."

"The more time I spent with Spencer, the clearer it became what a levelheaded, intelligent young man he is," said Jeanette on the voiceover. Then it cut back to Spencer outside the locker room right after Jeannette had pounced on him.

"How do you feel about all this?" Jeannette had asked him.

How did she think he felt? He had taken a deep breath. The overpowering floral scent of Jeannette's perfume made his eyes water.

"I think it's stupid. I mean, my birth certificate also says that I weighed seven pounds, but things change."

It cut to a clip of Spencer on the bench, watching the rest of the team play. The voiceover ended with Jeannette saying, "That's right, things change. And maybe it's time for the league's rules to change with our ever-evolving understanding of gender. This is Jeannette Perkins from channel seventeen. The evening news is next."

The program went to commercial. Spencer unclenched his fists, which he'd been holding so tight his fingernails tattooed half-moons in his palms. He took a shaky breath and glanced over to see his parents' reactions. Mom's hand was pressed against her mouth, and Dad was frowning, his lower lip jutting out in disappointment. For a second, Spencer thought he'd made a mistake doing the interview, but then Dad said, "Oh man, why did they cut my bit out?"

Spencer felt himself relax and laughed along with the rest of his family.

Twenty-two

The upcoming Monday, Spencer was more nervous than he had been his first day at Oakley. Mom and Dad had spent all weekend screening calls from reporters, supporters, and a few trolls. But Spencer had made his decision. It was like a can of refrigerator biscuits: impossible to put back in once opened.

Before he even got inside the building, he was ambushed by Macintosh, with Cory and Travis beside him. Spencer noticed that there was still no Justice.

"We're your bodyguards today," said Macintosh. "If anybody tries to give you shit, they'll have to go through us first."

"What about your classes?"

"Screw them."

Spencer had to admit, walking to his first class flanked by the guys was pretty cool. Less cool were the stares and whispers. When lunchtime came, he hightailed it to the QSA thinking he'd find peace among the queers.

When he opened the door and found the room dark and

empty, he thought maybe he had the day wrong. Then the lights came on and everyone jumped up from behind desks yelling, "Congratulations!"

Riley unfurled a banner that said *It's a boy!*

"What's all this?" asked Spencer, between bursts of laughter.

"We're throwing you a coming out party," said Riley. "I know you're already out, but we wanted to do something nice for you. It's not too cringey, is it?"

"This is super extra, but thanks." As he dug into a piece of blue cake, he thought more about his transition: coming out, his first therapy appointment, going on hormone blockers for the first time. He had treated each step as another obstacle to overcome. This was the first time he thought about it as something to be celebrated.

Halfway through lunch the door opened again and Principal Dumas walked in.

She examined the room. Her eyes fell on Spencer, whose brain thought the most appropriate response was to say "Would you like some cake?"

She smiled but shook her head. "I'm not staying long. I wanted to share that we've received your message about gender-neutral bathrooms loud and clear, and we appreciate the amount of work and effort it took for you all to do this. I want to assure you that we will consider your proposal very seriously.

"All I ask is for you to be patient. We'll need to find the money to build them and have those funds approved by the board, not to mention getting past building regulations and dealing with concerns from parents. But I'll do whatever I can to make Oakley more inclusive for students of all genders. Recent current events have shown me that being passive is going against progress."

The room erupted into claps and cheers once she left.

Grayson pulled Spencer aside. "I think you should see something."

"What?"

Grayson handed Spencer the petition. It was several pages longer than the last time Spencer had seen it. He recognized names from the boys' soccer team and the girls' soccer team, plus a whole bunch of names he didn't know.

"Did you get these signatures?"

Grayson shook his head. "That would be Justice. He dropped it off at my house last week, but I haven't seen him since."

Spencer considered sending Justice a text to say thanks but then he remembered that he no longer had Justice's number.

Spencer came home to a strange truck parked in the driveway. He walked inside to find a man in a cowboy hat sitting in the living room with his mom. The man stood to shake Spencer's hand.

"Paul Blankenship. I'm the league director. And you must be Spencer. You've caused quite a ruckus, I'll tell you what."

Spencer wasn't sure if he expected an apology, but he sure as hell wasn't going to give one, so he kept his mouth shut.

"Are you sure I can't get you anything to drink?" asked Mom.

"No ma'am, I'm here to see your boy." Mr. Blankenship hitched up his trousers and collapsed back in the armchair with a groan.

"Now, I'm an old-fashioned man. In my day, girls were girls and boys were boys. There wasn't any of this gender business." He waved his hand in a dismissive gesture, because obviously gender was something that had been made up in 2005. "However, I recognize that times have changed and you can either get with it or get left behind. Did you know that we were the first desegregated league in the state?" he said, as if he deserved a medal for not being racist.

"No, sir," said Spencer.

"It's true. Nobody can say that we aren't tolerant of others."

Spencer didn't want to be tolerated. You tolerated a bad smell. You tolerated a leaky faucet until it got fixed.

Mr. Blankenship continued, "I cannot tell you how many calls and emails we've received on your behalf. Your story certainly has sparked something in people. Therefore, we have agreed to revoke your ineligibility."

Spencer remained stunned for a moment as the words sunk in. Then he said, "You mean I can play?"

"That's correct."

"What about other trans kids?"

"We've talked it through, and we've decided to use *any* government-issued ID to determine gender."

It wasn't perfect, but it was still progress.

"And the tournament? Are we still eliminated?"

"The coach of the Wanderers has graciously bowed out. You're through to the finals."

Twenty-three

The day of the finals, Coach Schilling pulled Spencer into the hallway.

The door to the locker room shut behind him, muffling the sound of the team getting ready inside. Spencer's pregame jitters multiplied. What if there were protests? Or maybe the league reversed their decision and he wasn't going to be allowed to play.

"I've made a change to the lineup," said Coach. "I'm not starting you today."

Spencer blinked up at him. "But Coach—"

Coach Schilling raised his hand, stopping him. "Hear me out. Harlow's a physical side. Heck, they almost put one of my boys in the hospital last year. Your game fitness isn't there yet and I won't risk an injury. Plus, with Justice gone, I need you fresh for the second half."

Earlier that week, Coach had told them that Justice's father had pulled him from Oakley. Spencer rolled his lower lip between his teeth and bit down hard to stop it from wobbling.

Coach squeezed his neck gently. "I promise that you will

get a chance to play, so bottle up your feelings and save it for the field."

Spencer uncrossed his arms, drew himself up to his full height, and went back to join his team in the locker room.

Seventy-one minutes into the game, Coach Schilling kept his promise.

He placed both his hands on Spencer's shoulders. "I need you to help us rip through their defense."

Spencer nodded once. "Got it, Coach."

"We've got nineteen minutes to turn this game around. You know as well as I do that you belong on this team. Now go out there and show everyone else."

Spencer couldn't tell if it was the rush of blood in his ears blocking out the noise or if a hush fell across the stands.

The referee blew his whistle, and the crowd roared back to life. Chants of "Twinkle Toes" and "Go number eight!" swelled into a cacophony, surging through Spencer, firing him up.

When his foot crossed the white line, he was no longer a boy. He was a weapon.

For fifteen minutes Spencer pricked holes through the Harlow defense with his passes. He was almost untouchable.

His pass had already reached Micah when the Harlow captain smashed into him. He felt a sharp pain in his foot as the studs pierced through his boot. He fell to the ground.

The captain's face leered over him. "You should've stayed with the girls." He spat on the ground beside Spencer, then walked away.

Micah hoisted him to his feet and brushed grass clippings off his shoulder. "You all right?"

Spencer took a tentative step. A jolt of pain shot up his leg. He'd be sore in the morning, but he could still play. "I've felt worse."

The referee gave the Harlow captain a yellow card and awarded Oakley a free kick. Spencer shook his head to clear it. There was still a game to win.

"Micah, stand over there. I'm going to send the ball to you and you'll have an open goal. You can't miss."

"Are you sure?"

"You don't want to know how many hours of free kick footage I've watched. Trust me."

The referee blew his whistle. Spencer kicked the ball. A low groan passed through the Oakley fans in the stands, who thought he'd missed. But the ball landed where he intended, right at Micah's feet.

The Harlow players had crowded the box to defend against a free kick that never came. Instead it was Micah, unmarked, who released the ball like a torpedo. When the ball hit the back of the net, the cheers from the stand were so loud, someone on the street would've thought there was an explosion.

They were tied.

Spencer had never been so relieved to hear the referee's whistle at full time. For the second year in a row, the League Cup would be decided by penalties.

The team huddled around Coach Schilling. "Boys, I don't even have to say it. We don't need luck because luck is for the unprepared and we are more than prepared to win this game."

The Harlow captain stepped up to take the first penalty. He took a stuttering run. Macintosh dove, arms stretched out, and landed hard on his shoulder. The ball whizzed past his outstretched fingers and into the net.

Oakley: 0, Harlow: 1.

Macintosh stumbled to the sidelines clutching his shoulder.

"What's wrong?" asked Coach when he came into earshot.

Macintosh shook his head. "I tweaked it again." His face was white as a sheet.

Coach Schilling scrubbed a hand over his face. "Wrap it in ice. You're done."

"But Coach, I can play."

"I'm not risking it," he said firmly. He tipped his head back and sighed, then turned to the bench. "Cory, start warming up."

Cory turned whiter than Macintosh, if possible, but jumped off the bench.

Back on the pitch, it was Micah's turn to take a penalty.

His kick buried the ball in the net. All his practice had paid off.

Oakley: 1, Harlow: 1.

Cory lumbered across the field to stand between the sticks. As the next Harlow player stepped up, Spencer prayed that they would miss, if only to build Cory's confidence. Someone, somewhere must have heard, because the shot went inches wide.

Oakley: 1, Harlow: 1.

Then it was Oakley's turn. Wyatt's shot missed the net, bouncing off the goalpost instead. He kicked the ground in frustration.

The next Harlow player scored, making it Oakley: 1, Harlow: 2. They needed to score the next goal to stay in the game.

Luckily the Harlow goalie didn't stand a chance against Dylan. The ref blew his whistle, the goalie blinked, and the ball was in the net.

They were tied at two goals and one miss each.

Cory's hands shook after his last miss. The next kick was aimed at the top corner of the net. Cory's gloves grazed the ball, but it still went in.

As the next Oakley player's foot made contact with the ball, Spencer shut his eyes and didn't open them until cheers erupted from their side of the stadium. They were tied again, with one shot left each.

The last player for Harlow stepped up. Cory's eyes tracked him as he ran up to kick the ball. At the last second, Cory dove to the left, and landed on the ball. It was hard to tell who was more shocked that Cory had saved the shot, him or the other player.

They had one more chance. Spencer's shot was all that stood between them and the League Cup.

His legs trembled like Jell-O. The maw of the goal-mouth leered back at him. The referee blew his whistle. Spencer took a deep breath and ran toward the ball.

He knew statistically speaking that the bottom left corner was where the highest percentage of penalty kicks were scored, but he took a gamble, blasting the ball right down the center of the goal, and hoped it was the right one.

The goalie dove to the right and the ball swooshed in the net.

"That's my boy!" Dad's voice cut through the cheering crowd.

Spencer didn't even hear the final whistle. The team collapsed on top of him. Hands slapped his back and rubbed his head.

They had won.

Twenty-four

Every minute was better than the last. There were the big moments, like when he lifted the League Cup over his head before being drenched by Gatorade. There were the colossal moments, like when Cory showed Spencer an Instagram post from Rafi Sisa himself congratulating the team on their win.

Then there were the bittersweet moments, like when Justice's name was announced during the medal ceremony and Spencer had to remember how to breathe.

And finally there were the quiet moments, like when Spencer caught Coach Schilling looking down at the first medal he'd won in his thirty years of coaching with the face one might have when cradling a baby bird. Their eyes locked across the pitch; a ripple of gratitude flowed between them.

That evening, more than a dozen mud-covered, grass-stained boys crowded into a greasy diner, cramming into booths and sprawling across tables. There was a constant flurry of activity near the kitchen as harried servers bustled in and out, balancing trays piled high with mountains of hamburgers.

Coach Schilling dinged his cup with a fork, but the dull clink was drowned out by a shriek as someone emptied an entire pitcher of pop over Cory's head.

"Listen up," called Macintosh, his arm in a sling. A final torrent of curse words poured from Cory's mouth, then everyone was quiet.

Coach Schilling scanned the room. "I started this year a broken man, but coaching this team has put me back together."

Micah began chanting, "Schil-ling, Schil-ling," until Coach put up his hands to stop him.

"That said, this is my last season of being your coach."

Spencer's heart plummeted, joining the burgers and fries in his stomach. His own shock was reflected in the stunned faces around him. Nobody spoke until a server tripped over Cory's duffel bag, clattering dishes to the ground. Then the team buried Coach under an avalanche of questions.

"Where are you going?"

"Will there still be a soccer team?"

"What about next year?"

"Listen," said Coach Schilling. "You didn't win because of me. Your victory was earned through the courage and dedication each of you displayed this season. I have no doubt in my mind that this team will go on to do great things, with or without me. For now, let's enjoy tonight."

· · ·

Spencer was still so filled with adrenaline when he got home that he didn't think he would be able to sleep. Still, he changed into his pajamas and climbed into bed. A few minutes later, all thoughts of sleeping went out the window when he got a text from an unknown number.

All it said was: *Meet me in the tree house.*

Justice. It had to be.

Twenty-five

Spencer slipped on sweatpants, tiptoed downstairs, and slid open the back door.

His pulse climbed with each rung of the ladder. When he reached the top, he saw Justice silhouetted in the darkness. He pulled himself up onto the platform and crouched in the opposite corner of the tree house. They eyed each other like two feral tomcats.

Justice broke the silence. "Congratulations. You played well."

Spencer let out a hollow laugh. "I had to. You weren't there."

The wounded look that flashed across Justice's face almost made him regret saying it. Almost.

"I'm sorry. I wanted to be there, but my dad wouldn't let me go."

Some of the anger he felt toward Justice ebbed away. "Because of me?"

"Martha heard everything on Halloween. After you left,

she gave me an ultimatum and told me that I had to tell my parents about me being gay or she would."

"Shit, are you okay?" He reached out an arm to touch Justice, but stopped himself. "How are you so calm about this?"

Justice turned away. "Because the worst has happened and I'm still here."

"Yeah, but—"

"Now my family knows, even if they are in denial about it."

Any residual anger he'd felt toward Justice was replaced by guilt. "This is my fault. None of this would've happened if—"

Justice edged forward, reducing the gap between them. "No, you don't understand. I never thought this would be possible. I thought maybe I could come out in college, but then, being an out athlete isn't exactly easy either, so that would be another four years of being in the closet. Another four years wasted. I'm done with hiding."

Being in such close proximity to Justice but not touching him ached like pressing on a day-old bruise.

"If you're not coming back to Oakley . . . is this goodbye?"

"Sort of. You remember the guy from the U.S. Youth Soccer Academy?"

"Yeah," said Spencer, unsure what it had to do with anything.

"He wants Coach for the under-eighteen national team."

So that explained the mystery of why Coach was leaving.

"But Coach said he'd take the job on one condition."

"What's that?" Spencer wondered why Justice was bringing this up now.

"That I'd go with him."

"What did you say?" he asked in a whisper.

"That I'd ask my parents."

"What did your parents say?"

"They couldn't say no to a full scholarship. Plus one less mouth to feed, and Noble could have his own room. Dad thinks it will 'toughen me up.'"

Spencer wished he could kiss away the pained look on Justice's face. "When are you going?"

"They want me to start training immediately. We're leaving first thing tomorrow."

Spencer felt his world come apart, but he managed a watery smile. "Well, congratulations. I guess you're getting out of Apple Creek."

Justice rubbed the back of his neck. "The thing is, I don't think I can do this without you. I know it will be difficult with the distance and all, but—" Justice broke off.

The silence that followed felt like an eternity.

"I want to be your boyfriend. If you'll have me back."

Spencer shoved Justice roughly against the wall of the tree house. Justice's eyes widened in surprise. His pulse fluttered beneath Spencer's fingertips. Spencer kissed Justice so hard, their teeth clanged against each other.

"Is that a yes?" Justice asked, voice hoarse.

In response, Spencer dove in for another kiss.

When the cold had turned his lips too numb to feel Justice's kisses, Spencer snuck him inside and up to his bedroom.

They lay on his bed, Justice running his fingers through Spencer's curls. His eyelids grew heavy and he let himself be rocked gently by the steady rise and fall of Justice's breathing.

Spencer was just drifting off to sleep when Justice spoke again. "You know that thing Coach always wears?"

"The hoodigan?" Spencer kept his eyes closed.

"Oh, I called it the cardihood." Justice's body rumbled against Spencer as he chuckled. "I asked him why he wore it to every game. You know what he said?"

"A good-luck charm?" said Spencer sleepily.

"No, fashion." Justice's body shook with laughter and soon Spencer joined in. He squeezed Justice tight, memorizing his body, his laugh, never wanting it to end.

Twenty-six

The next few days were measured by everyday acts of courage from Spencer and his family.

The first act came Monday morning when Spencer, Theo, and Mom waited on the curb for the school bus. Theo's eyes, round as soccer balls, peeked out from under his hat. Snowflakes settled on his long eyelashes.

The school bus tore around the corner and rumbled down the street.

"Maybe I'll wait until tomorrow," said Theo, his voice muffled by a thick scarf.

Spencer crouched to Theo's height. "I know it's scary, but you can do this."

"We'll be right behind you, I promise," said Mom.

The bus sputtered to a halt in front of them and the doors hissed opened, like the gaping mouth of a kid-eating monster.

Theo took a deep breath, puffed out his cheeks, then let it all out in a white plume.

"Ready?" said Spencer, adjusting Theo's headphones.

Theo's foot hesitated above the first step.

"You've got this, little man," said Spencer.

Theo climbed the rest of the way onto the bus. The doors closed behind him, swallowing him up.

"He'll be all right, won't he?" said Mom, voice wavering.

Spencer rested his hand on her shoulder, realizing with a burst of satisfaction that he was almost as tall as her. That was new.

"He's going to be more than all right. And if he's not, we'll be there to pick up the pieces."

They got into the Subaru, which had been idling in the driveway. Fat snowflakes melted on the windshield as the bus roared to life and they followed it down the street.

"You know," said Mom. "Now that you're settled and Theo's older, I might go back to work."

"Nursing?"

"I was thinking advocacy. We're so fortunate, but there are many families who aren't."

"You can use your nursing background to school idiots who lie about things like how hormone blockers work," said Spencer with a smile.

"That too. What do you think?"

"I think it's a great idea. You might need a bigger bullet journal, though."

. . .

The second act of courage came on Friday.

Spencer stared at the papers on the podium in front of him as the wind ruffled his hair and whipped at his jacket. Overhead, clouds loomed heavy above the football field like lead balloons.

He had written and rewritten his speech for Transgender Day of Remembrance, ignoring Mom's offer to help. This was something he had to do on his own. Well, not exactly on his own. Riley was to his right and Grayson was to his left. The rest of the QSA fanned out behind him.

Spencer took a deep breath and leaned into the microphone.

"When I first came to Oakley, my biggest concern wasn't if I was going to make friends or if I would get good grades. What I was most anxious about was using the bathroom. Transgender people like me are often told where we can and can't go. Newsflash: Everybody pees." A rumble of laughter came from the bleachers where the rest of the school huddled under coats and umbrellas.

He continued, "I didn't realize it then, but I do now. It isn't about bathrooms, just like the civil rights movement wasn't about water fountains or seats on a bus. Denying someone a basic human right is another way to dehumanize them. Unfortunately, transgender people experience injustices like this and worse every day, especially transgender women of color."

Spencer held up a thick stack of paper. "This is a list of every transgender person killed so far this year. In observance of Transgender Day of Remembrance tomorrow, we're going to honor them and their lives."

The frigid air numbed his fingers, causing him to struggle lighting his match. Riley stepped forward and helped him light his candle. Spencer shot them a grateful smile.

Riley held their candle to Spencer's until the wick sparked and ignited, then Grayson did the same. All around him, candles lit up, illuminating the stands with a warm, flickering light.

There was a clap of thunder. Spencer's hair crackled with static electricity. Up above, the sky was like a bruise: all deep blues, grays, and purples.

When the first name floated off his tongue like a prayer, the sky opened up in response. Rain fell in sheets, pummeling the football field, pinging off the bleachers, and soaking through Spencer's jacket.

With each name he read, the storm grew in strength.

He was halfway through the list when the power cut out on his microphone. He tried to keep going, but the wind was too loud. The people he was honoring had already been silenced in life. He couldn't let them be silenced in death as well.

A flash of color from the bleachers caught his eye. It was Ms. Hart, dressed in a bright skirt. This gave Spencer an idea. He motioned for Grayson and Riley to come closer.

"I need your help. If I say the name, will you repeat it and get everyone around you to repeat it until it reaches everybody in the stands?"

Grayson nodded. "We'll do it. We'll amplify your voice."

Spencer read the names as loud as he could. They echoed around the bleachers until the voices of the living drowned out the roaring thunder with the names of the dead.

His throat was raw when he reached the end of the list. As the last name left his lips, the rain stopped, the sky cleared, and all was calm.

Justice's pixelated face grinned at Spencer through his laptop screen. "That sounds amazing. I wish I could've been there."

Spencer had just finished telling him how Transgender Day of Remembrance had gone that afternoon. "Theo filmed it. Hang on, you're stuck."

He took advantage of the frozen screen to stare at Justice's face, his mouth open in mid-laugh. Between their busy schedules, it was tough to find time to talk since Justice had left a couple weeks before. But they texted every day after school and squeezed in video time on the weekend between Justice's games.

"Okay, you're back."

"I'm so proud of you," said Justice.

Spencer swallowed hard, his throat suddenly dry. "How's the academy?" he asked, changing the subject.

"Intense. They've got me on a strict training schedule to get into shape. They don't play around here. But I'm learning a lot. I miss you, though," he said, his voice soft as velvet.

"I miss you too. I've got everything ready for Thanksgiving. Picture this: popcorn, candy, and over eleven hours of *Lord of the Rings*."

Justice groaned. "You're lucky I like you so much."

Dad poked his head in. "You've got a few more minutes, bud, then lights-out." He spotted Spencer's laptop screen. "Oh, are you talking to Justice?" He shoved his big old head in front of the screen. "What's going on, my man?"

"Hi, Professor Harris. Sorry for keeping Spencer awake."

"It's no problem. You winning up there?"

"I'm doing my best."

"We're going to see you next week at Thanksgiving, right? You haven't lived until you've tried my mac and cheese."

"Yep, Coach and I are coming after our last match. He wanted to know if we should bring anything."

"Just yourselves. You know Connie and I are happy to have you whenever you need a break or anything."

Spencer looked away while Justice swiped a hand over his eyes. "Thanks, Professor Harris," he said thickly.

"Of course. Well, I'll let you two say your good nights. Good luck on your game."

Spencer locked eyes with Justice, and at the same time they said, "Luck is for the unprepared," before bursting into laughter. Dad shook his head as he left the room and closed the door behind him.

Eventually, they stopped laughing and Spencer stared at the screen. He felt his heart swell in his chest. "Hey, Justice?"

"Yeah?"

"I lo—" The door of Justice's room opened and Justice's roommate came in with a towel wrapped around his waist.

"Hey man, sorry, are you busy?"

Justice rolled his eyes to Spencer on the camera. "Just talking with my boyfriend."

"Cool, cool." His roommate began searching for his clothes, his towel slipping slightly.

Before he'd left, Justice had decided that he wasn't going to make a huge deal about being out, but if people asked, he'd tell them he was gay and had a boyfriend. So far nobody had a problem with it.

Justice looked back at Spencer. He sighed. "I should go."

"Okay."

"Were you trying to say something before?"

In the background, he could hear Justice's roommate singing along to Taylor Swift.

Spencer shook his head. What he'd wanted to say could wait. He'd have another chance. Hopefully many chances. For now, this was more than enough.

Acknowledgments

First, thank you to the Pitch Wars community, especially my mentor, Natalka Burian, for wrangling a sprawling mess of random plotlines into a story.

A huge thank-you to my agent, Jordan Hamessley, for being a fierce champion of that story from day one.

To my editor, Ellen Cormier, who guided me through breaking that story and putting it back together again with such insight and care.

And thanks, too, to everyone at Dial and Penguin who worked so hard to take that story and turn it into this book. And to Xavier Schipani for the beautiful cover illustration that ties it all together.

To the following authors who have lent their support—Adalyn Grace, Aden Polydoros, Adib Khorram, Aiden Thomas, Jackson Bird, Julian Winters, Kacen Callender, Mason Deaver, Phil Stamper, Victoria Lee, and Zabé Ellor.

Thank you to Pep Guardiola and the players at Manchester City for the fantastic football.

And thanks to everyone who has showered me with their love and friendship, which I have poured back into every page of this book— Della Connelly, Raquel Toledo, Rebecca, Charles & Lily Fitzsimons, my other families across the pond and across the river, and the loved ones I keep in my heart, Neal Fitzsimons and Jay Carr.

Finally, to Aiden Rivera Schaeff, for showing me what was possible when I didn't even know what I was looking for. Thank you.